DATE DUE

APR 05 1994			
APR 27 1994			
MAY 10 1996			

Is Anybody There?

IS ANYBODY THERE?

a novel by

Eve Bunting

HarperCollinsPublishers

Is Anybody There?

Printed in the United States of America. For information address HarperCollins Children's Books, a division of HarperCollins Publishers, 10 East 53rd Street, New York, N.Y. 10022.
Typography by Joyce Hopkins
5 6 7 8 9 10

Library of Congress Cataloging-in-Publication Data
Bunting, Eve, date
Is anybody there?

Summary: After discovering the disappearance of several household items, Marcus, a thirteen-year-old latchkey child, suspects that a stranger may be prowling around inside his house while he's at school and his mother is at work.
[1. Latchkey children—Fiction. 2. Mothers and sons—Fiction] I. Title.
PZ7.B91527Ir 1988 [Fic] 87-45881
ISBN 0-397-32302-6
ISBN 0-397-32303-4 (lib. bdg.)

For my father,
Sloan E. Bolton.
Thanks.

CHAPTER 1

It was the week before Christmas when I first got the idea that someone was watching our house.

My name is Marcus Mullen. I'm thirteen years old, and I don't usually wimp out over just nothing. What made my creepy, crawly, eyes-on-the-back-of-my-neck feeling so silly was that it was morning. I mean, it wasn't even a dark and stormy night. The sun was shining and I was standing at the end of our driveway waiting for my friend, Robbie, to come by so we could walk to school together, the way we always do. The sky was a deep, calm blue. The thermometer on the porch said 76 degrees, typical for December 20 in Southern California. Mom had left for work already. I'd made sure the house was safely locked, and my key hidden where I always hide it, on a nub of the oak tree by the back door.

In other words, it was an ordinary morning. So why was I getting this weird feeling? I began an off-key whistle and turned a slow 360 degrees. The tall oleander hedge that grows between our house and the house next door where Miss Sarah and Miss Coriander Clark live was atwitter with small, busy birds. At the end of our driveway is the upstairs apartment, which Nick, our tenant, rents. I'd seen him leave for work already in his little green Dodge. Nick teaches phys. ed. and coaches football at La Costa High. His door was closed, his miniblinds tightly shut. I get bad vibes even thinking about Nick and the way he and my mom have started moon gazing at each other, so I let myself look past his apartment, skimming over our house to the neighbor's roof on the other side. The roof is all you can see from here because of the oak tree and the thick shrubbery that Nick says he's going to thin out one of these days. He takes care of the garden as part of his rent. I turned some more. On the other side of the street the Dellarosa house stood quietly in the sun. Nobody was watching me from there. Not even their old dog, Patchin, was in sight.

I stopped whistling. Of course nobody was watching me. I gave my shoulders a little shake and began jogging in place. Then I saw Robbie coming around the corner from Sherwood, where he lives, and I rushed to meet him. I didn't say anything about the creepies I'd had while I waited. What was there to say, anyway? Actually, I almost forgot about my feeling. It wasn't until later, thinking back, that I remembered it began that morning.

The last day of school before Christmas vacation is always great. I decided not to spoil it worrying about something that was probably all in my imagination. Ms. Hansen, our teacher, let us play a bunch of games—like Heads Up, Seven Up and Benjamin Franklin—and then she read us the end of *The Best Christmas Pageant Ever.* It's a funny story, and she'd timed it just right so we'd have the last chapter on the last day. We were getting into what Ms. Hansen calls a "meaningful discussion" about the book when the bell rang.

"Everybody go quietly now to the

cafetorium," Ms. Hansen shouted over the din. "And please behave nicely during the performance. That means you, too, Robbie Roberts."

Robbie rolled his eyes. "Yes, Ms. Hansen." He turned to me. "Can you believe we're going to have the Pacific High School Christmas Program *again* this year?" We have had the Pacific High School Program every Christmas through elementary school and even kindergarten. "If they do 'Rudolf the Red-Nosed Reindeer' one more time, I'm going to throw up," Robbie told me.

Anjelica Trotter nodded. "Really! Especially if that guy comes prancing out with his nose all lit up." She groaned a great groan; Robbie and I pretended we didn't hear.

Anjelica Trotter has become a total pain. I don't know what her problem is. She's always hanging around Robbie and me, especially me. She wears a ton of makeup and she has I LOVE SOMEBODY printed in big letters on the spine of her notebook. Every time she sees me in the halls or at the lockers, she holds up the notebook and smiles. I guess I'm supposed to figure I'm the "somebody." It's weird, because right up through sixth grade Anjelica was OK. She didn't wear makeup or anything, and I used to kind of like her, to tell the truth. I don't like her anymore. At least, I don't think I do.

"What kind of lipstick is that you're wearing, Anjelica?" Robbie asked her. It was some strange stuff all right, a mixture of green and red.

"Like it?" Anjelica asked Robbie, batting her eyes at me. "It's called 'Color Me Christmas.' "

"It looks as if you've been sucking on a candy cane," Robbie said.

"It *is* peppermint flavor," Anjelica told me, although I wasn't the one who'd asked.

I swear Anjelica has gotten really spaced. Robbie says it's because her hormones are growing up too, but I think she's flipped out. She even came to my house one day after school. I'd been working in our garage on the bike I'm making Mom for Christmas, and when I opened our front door and saw Anjelica Trotter there, I just about died.

"I found your math book on a bench in the playground," Anjelica said. "I thought you might need it, so I brought it over."

"Oh, thanks." I felt my face going white. "It

would have been OK tomorrow, though. We don't have math homework."

"I know. I just thought you might want to study." She'd raised her four eyebrows. I wasn't sure four was the fashion now or if she'd made a mistake trying to darken her own.

"Can I come in?" she asked.

For some reason I was really scared of letting Anjelica into my house. "Well, it's just . . ." I was half closing the door. "My mom's not home from work and I'm not supposed to let anybody in if I don't have permission. It's a kind of rule. Thanks a lot though for the book." I'd smiled a fake smile and added, "Would you like some lemonade? I could bring it out."

"No thanks," Anjelica huffed.

"Thanks again," I called as she got on her bike.

It's truly astonishing that Anjelica still seems to like me after that. Robbie says I was very impolite that day, not to mention chicken.

Anjelica was sitting beside me now at the Pacific High School Christmas Program and I think she was wearing the same perfume that had blasted at me that day by my front door. The show was pretty good, even though there was a guy in the front row of the chorus who kept grinning down at us and stroking his skimpy mustache. I kept trying to look somewhere else. Still, the show was OK. The whole day was OK. We had turkey burritos and cranberry juice for lunch and only one class afterward, where we did hardly anything.

The minute the last bell rang everyone started shouting "Merry Christmas" and "See you next year!" which sounds a long time away but is really only a couple of weeks. Robbie and I managed to escape Anjelica, who was standing by the door holding a wizened piece of twig that she said was mistletoe. She waved it over the head of any guy she could catch, and Anjelica is pretty quick. There were an awful lot of guys with red-and-green smears on their faces. Robbie and I snuck through the gym and out the side gate.

"Are you sure you don't want to . . ." Robbie began, but I squashed him with a look. I felt like one of those calves in cowboy movies that has just escaped the branding iron.

"Have you noticed how much Anjelica's top has grown these last few days?" Robbie asked me as we walked home.

"I don't notice anything about Anjelica Trotter," I told him, which wasn't true.

"I think she's got something stuffed in there," Robbie whispered. "She just about grew overnight."

"Maybe that happens," I said. "Like toenails. My mom's always telling me to cut mine, and I—"

Robbie shook his head. "A top couldn't grow that quick. Last Tuesday there was nothing. On Wednesday . . . Who knows how big it will be by next *year*!"

I was glad we were almost at my house. Sometimes when Robbie starts talking about girl parts he doesn't know when to stop.

"Want to come in for a minute?" I asked.

"Naw. I'm supposed to be rushing home. I'll call you tomorrow."

"See you." I started walking toward the house, and suddenly I began peering this way and that. Crazy! I never get scared around here.

Nick's car wasn't in the driveway. Probably

he was still at school. Even though football season's over, I'll bet Nick still has his guys working out. He's really gung ho. Nick must be some coach, I have to give him that. Robbie's cousin, Jimmy, is on the team, and he says he is. This is the first time the La Costa Cougars have ever gone all the way to the championships. They were on TV and there was big, old Nick being interviewed, filling the screen, saying he'd had a bunch of fine young men to work with and they deserved all the credit. I told Mom I didn't think that was a very original remark, and she asked me what I meant, and I said I only meant that coaches always say that and I thought Nick could have come up with something better.

"What is there to say that's better than that?" she asked quietly, and turned away.

I squinted up at his apartment now. When Mom had advertised it last spring, Nick was the first to show. He took it right away. Who wouldn't? The apartment is like a little tower sitting on its own at the top of a flight of stairs, like a crow's nest or a lighthouse. I wouldn't mind living in that apartment myself.

Nick had planted a new winter lawn in front,

green and lush. Our house looks nice too, all decorated for the holidays, although of course the Christmas lights are not turned on right now. Last weekend Mom and I put up the strings of colored balls above the porch, parallel to the roof. Nick was home, and I was surprised he didn't come down to help. But afterward I thought maybe Mom told him that she and I have always done this together since Dad died and suggested Nick stay away. We also have a tree with lights in the living room, but we don't hang the Christmas ornaments on it until Christmas Eve.

I took a sniff of the warm air that smelled of sun on fresh-cut grass. Who needs pine trees and cold anyway? This is Christmas.

I went around the back, dropped my blue nylon book bag by the live oak tree and ducked under for my key. It's dim in there and you can barely see, but my hand knows its way. I felt for the little nub and found it. Then I pushed aside leaves and twigs, peering at the trunk. The nub was empty. The key was gone.

CHAPTER 2

I came out from under the shade of the tree and my creepy feeling was back in full force. In the five years since Dad died, since Mom went back to work and I'd been a latchkey kid, I'd always been able to reach in under that tree and find my key exactly where I'd left it. What could have happened to it? Had someone taken it? Had someone been watching me this morning?

My eyes jumped all around, to the thick shrubbery on the right, to the oleander hedge on the left. I backed up against the house, turned to face the sun-warm wall, and pressed myself small against it. Was someone inside? Sweat trickled down my chest and back.

There had to be a simple explanation. Mom was home. That was it. I slid along the wall to the back door and tried the handle. Locked. So? She would lock it from the inside. She always locks the house.

"Mom?" I called, but not very loudly, just in case she wasn't the one.

A UPS package sat on the mat. The guy always leaves packages back here so no one can see them from the front. My aunt Charlie's writing was on the label, and normally I would have shaken the parcel and tried to guess what she'd sent for Christmas. But this wasn't normally. I leaned against the wall. About a million ants climbed in a black line two inches from my shoulder. I didn't move.

After a minute I snaked out my hand and rang the doorbell. Over the pounding of my heart I heard it *ding dong, ding dong* inside the house. Now Mom would come, and she'd say, "Oh, Marky, you know what? I locked . . . couldn't find . . . left my key. . . ." But wouldn't Mom have taken in the package? I slid farther from the door, wishing now I hadn't rung the bell.

Nobody came.

Maybe there was a burglar in there, ripping us off. Everybody knows Christmas is a favorite time for burglars. He'd seen me hide the key and . . . OK, now, Marcus. Don't panic. Maybe Mom gave the key to Nick. Maybe he needed to get in the house for some reason and she'd said: "Here! But be sure to put it back for Marcus. He'll need it after school." Sure, that's what it was. And Nick had forgotten. I could kill that guy, Nick.

I tiptoed around the house and raced up the stairs to his apartment, looking over my shoulder all the time at our silent house below. Nobody came when I knocked. Nick had hung a plastic Christmas wreath on the door, with red plastic apples and berries sticking on it. I hate plastic wreaths, but I guess they're like plastic Christmas trees, very practical.

"Come on, come on," I whispered. "This time be here." After a minute I tried the knob, and the door opened. Dumb! That's dumb, Nick. Don't you know there are thieves around at this time of year?

He'd fixed the place up nice, all right. There was a big picture of some kind of flying bird on the wall. But all I cared about was that the place was empty. Nick wasn't here. Well, sure. If I'd been thinking right I'd have remembered that his car wasn't parked below either. But then I wasn't thinking right. Nick was back at school, then, with my key in his pocket . . . maybe.

I was just about to back out when I saw the photograph lying on the wicker table by the door. It was black and white, about the size of a page from my school notebook. Even though I was seeing it upside down I knew who it was. I stood looking down at it without touching it.

Mom. Mom sitting in the kitchen. Her elbows were on the table and she had her special mug cupped in her hands. Her eyes were sad, as if she was remembering something far, far away. Her shoulders drooped. Her hair half hid her face. I knew it was a wonderful picture. It captured a longing in her that she kept hidden, one that made my throat close up with my own sadness. She hadn't known it was being taken, but whoever took it loved her. I closed Nick's door and ran back down the steps. Ran where? Not back to the house.

I crouched behind Nick's wooden stairs for a minute, trying to think, trying to leave the sad image of Mom and get myself back together. After a couple of minutes I squeezed through the oleander hedge and into the Clarks' yard.

Across the street Patchin had come slowly into his front yard and stood, stiff legged, pretending to watch me. Patchin is so old I doubt if he can even see across the street. Last week Mrs. Dellarosa had opened his mouth to show me he has no teeth anymore. Some guard dog.

Miss Coriander came to the back door before I could knock. I like her better than Miss Sarah. She has gray hair pulled back, and the whitest white skin, without a single wrinkle. She's stooped about double, and she peers up at you as she talks. I think that's one reason why she and Miss Sarah don't miss anything. Miss Coriander sees all that goes on at her level, and Miss Sarah is tall and keeps watch up above. Miss Coriander's eyes are blue, but Miss Sarah has one blue and one brown, both sharp. If there'd been anything or anybody to see around our house, Miss Coriander or Miss Sarah Clark would have seen it, or him.

"Good afternoon, Marcus," Miss Coriander said.

"Hi. Did you happen to . . . to see someone at our back door today?" I asked.

"No. Why?" Matching eyes can be sharp too.

"I just—"

"Speak up, Marcus. Is something wrong?"

I'd have to be careful here. Miss Sarah and Miss Coriander are pretty disapproving of Mom leaving me alone.

"What do you expect me to do?" Mom had asked them. "I have to work."

"He could stay with *us*, Caroline."

Oh wow! Mom and I had had a meaningful discussion. But if Mom knew about *this*, I'd be back to square one.

"I just wondered," I said vaguely.

"Sarah!" When Miss Coriander raises her voice, she really raises it. Miss Sarah came in a flash. "Did you see anybody at the Mullens' house today, Sarah?"

Miss Sarah pulled off her gardening gloves. "I saw that young man, Nick," she said. "He came down the steps and got in his car. He was wearing those short khaki shorts and that tight white T-shirt."

"That's what he wears to his *job*," I said,

wondering why I was bothering to defend Nick, especially now that I knew about the photograph.

"Didn't that dog of the Dellarosas bark some today?" Miss Coriander asked.

"Oh, him!" Miss Sarah dismissed Patchin with a wave of her hand.

"And why are you asking about someone at the house, Marcus?"

So they hadn't seen anything. I had to think fast or they'd worm the whole story out of me, and call Mom right in the middle of her Christmas rush, and she'd have to come home and . . . I'd have to tell Mom myself, anyway. A missing key is dangerous stuff. But *I'd* tell her, not them. It would be the same thing if I asked to borrow their emergency key. There'd be questions and a lecture about responsibility and more suggestions to Mom.

"Someone left a gift by the door," I said. "That's all. I thought you might have seen who it was."

"Someone left a gift?" Miss Coriander cast an accusing glance at Miss Sarah. "How did you miss that, Sarah?"

"It must have been while I was at the market. You weren't keeping an eye out, Coriander."

I began edging away. "I guess I'll find out at Christmas," I said. "No sweat. Just checking."

Now I couldn't wait to go back and look some more for the key because I'd just thought of something. What a relief! The key could have fallen off the nub. Of course that was what had happened. I'd told myself not to panic, but I hadn't listened. Easy now to imagine myself hanging it up this morning on its loop of worn tape, to imagine it swinging gently, dropping. Or maybe . . .

"Was there a big wind today?" I asked Miss Sarah.

She gave me one of her sharp, double-barreled blue-brown stares. "Wind? What is all this about? What are you up to, Marcus?"

"Nothing, honest, Miss Sarah." I had backed myself partway through the oleander hedge. "Well, see you!" I was in our yard now, running in my new, zigzag, crouched position across the front of the house toward the live oak tree. Miss Sarah and Miss Coriander wouldn't miss this strange maneuver. "What's he up to *now*?" Miss Sarah would ask. "Isn't Marcus too old to still be playing army?"

I stood in the shade of the tree, panting a bit before I got down on my hands and knees. It was gloom and doom down here. I wished I had our big flashlight. But the flashlight was in the house, and the house was locked, and I didn't have the key. . . . Catch-22, as Mom always says. My hands kept finding things among the dead leaves that I didn't even want to think about. I was sure by its shape that this one was either a very small pinecone or a piece of dried-up dog poop. Probably poop. Probably Patchin's. Well, better Patchin's than a strange dog's.

Lots of gross-feeling things down there, but no key.

I stood up, bumping my head, and then I saw the small shine of metal as a ray of sun slanted in. I peered closer. There was the key. I stared at it for the longest time. It was hanging from a sticking-out nub, all right. But this was the wrong nub.

CHAPTER 3

I wasn't sure what to do next, so I stood, telling myself that I must have put the key back in the wrong place. But I didn't believe it. Then I decided that it still had to be Nick. Easier to blame him than me anyway.

I saw his car right at that minute turning into our driveway, coming to a stop below his apartment.

"Speak of the devil," I said. "Old Nick himself!"

I came out from under the tree and walked across the grass. "Hi," I said. The key was hidden, sharp and warm in my closed fist.

"Hi, Marcus. You just get here?"

"Just about."

He was leaning into the back of the car bringing out a box with "Two Dozen Multicolored Christmas Lights" printed on it.

"I promised your mom I'd get a set of these on my way home. She thought the tree was kind of bare."

"Oh." She hadn't mentioned to *me* that the tree was kind of bare. When did she and Nick have these private conversations? And when had he taken that photograph?

Nick headed around the house, and I walked a pace behind him.

"It's locked," I said when he stopped at the door.

"You have your key?" he asked. I nodded, but kept my fist closed. Without saying anything else Nick took his keys from his pocket and put one in the lock, and the door opened.

"You have a key to our house?" I asked, trying not to sound the way I felt. Actually, I wasn't sure what way I felt. One thing, though. If he had his own key, he didn't need mine.

He glanced down at me. "Your mom gave it to me. In case I need to do laundry when there's no one home, stuff like that." He moved to one side. "Come on in."

"Gee, thanks." I didn't bother to disguise my sarcasm. Where did he get off inviting me into my own house?

I picked up my backpack and Aunt Charlie's package and stepped past him. But just inside the door I stopped. "Wait a sec, Nick."

I was listening, listening hard but hearing nothing. It made no sense anyway. If someone had been here, they'd gone already. If someone had been here, they'd used the key and put it back.

"What are we waiting *for*?" Nick asked.

I shrugged, glancing around the kitchen. Everything looked normal. I set the parcel and my backpack on the table.

"I thought I heard a noise," I said to Nick. "This time of year, you know . . . the house empty . . . sometimes people try to get in and rip stuff off."

Nick bent to look into my face, which I made carefully blank, then put a hand between my shoulder blades. "Well, let's just check."

I liked it that he didn't give me any bull. I liked it that he didn't sound fake cheerful either, the way you'd be with a little kid who thought there was a monster in the closet. I guess most teachers are psychologists too.

We went from room to room, and I have to admit it was nice having Nick there. Who's going to jump out from under a bed and tackle a big guy like this one?

The house was calm and quiet, filled with the comforting warmth of sunlight. Mom had put some white camellias in a glass jar on her bedside table, and one of the petals fell with a plop and a dusting of pollen.

"Nobody here," I said.

We have a laundry room with a toilet and washbasin. Nick opened the door to look inside. A narrow flight of uncarpeted steps from the laundry room led to our half-finished attic.

"I'll just check above too," he said, and I nodded.

"Why not?"

Our attic's full of old boxes, the trunk Dad had when he went away to college, the old cedar chest, and cobwebs.

When Nick was partway up the steps, he opened the hatch that was the attic door, and then all I could see were his furry legs, his white socks, and his white Nikes.

"Nothing there." He edged back down, closing the hatch behind him. "It must have been Santa and his elves you heard."

"I guess so." I hadn't realized my stomach

was knotted until it relaxed on me. So I had simply hung that key on the wrong nub this morning. OK. I followed Nick back into the living room and watched as he clipped the new lights on the tree.

"That's better," he said when he turned them on. I thought so too, even though I'd thought there were enough before.

"Mom should have asked me," I muttered, but Nick didn't answer. He paused on the way back through the kitchen.

"Do you mind being alone, Marcus? You can come up with me, you know."

"I don't mind. Actually I like being alone," I added.

"Yes. That's what your mom tells me."

So she'd told him that, had she?

Then Nick opened the door into the garage and switched on the light. I guess when this guy checks a place, he really checks it.

Looking past him I could see the workbench, my bike on its kickstand, the drape hiding Mom's present, and all my bike junk in a pile in the corner. I could see the oil spot shaped like Australia on the floor. Robbie and I had put in red blobs for Perth and Sydney and Oodnadatta, a town Robbie had found in the middle of the map of Australia. He said he liked the sound of it. There was nobody hiding in the garage either.

"Get your Campies yet?" Nick asked.

"No."

The Campagnolo pedals were all I needed to finish Mom's bike. They were on order in Henry's Bike Shop, but they hadn't come in yet. I hated it that Nick knew about them and about Mom's present. I hadn't meant to share the secret, but he'd come into the garage one day while I was working on the bike so I'd had to tell. He'd walked all around it, admiring it, and I could see he was really amazed that I'd built it from scratch. Actually, Nick's always nice to me. That's not the problem. The problem is I'm happy here, by myself and with Mom. And I don't want him trying to get in good with her by getting in good with me. Not that he seems to be having any trouble getting in good with her. She'd even given him a *key*!

"Have you tried the other bike shops in town for the Campies?" Nick asked. "You might luck out."

"I'm going to check Henry's again tomorrow," I said. "He thought they'd be in. Thanks for the lights. And for the house search. I feel kind of stupid."

"No need."

Nick sounded fatherly, and if there's one thing I'm not in the market for, it's a father. "How much do we owe you for the lights?" I asked, reminding him that all he is here is a paying tenant.

"No need for that either." I couldn't figure out the look he gave me.

"See you," he said.

I walked straight into the hall when he left, got the blackthorn stick that used to be my father's, and went over the house again myself. This time I checked to see if anything was missing, because somebody might have been in here. It wasn't likely, but still . . . We didn't have sterling silver, but Mom's silver plate was all there in the sideboard drawer. The dimes she collects in a green glass jar seemed to be at the same level.

I stood in the silence of her bedroom. She has a Chinese jewel box, which locks with a brass key that she keeps in the drawer under her panty hose. I found the key, opened the box, and went over her valuables, one by one. There aren't that many and they were all there: the pin set in pearls that Grandma had given her; her garnet earrings—my dad had bought her those on their fifth anniversary; his gold watch.

I took it out and held it against my wrist. The watch will be mine when I'm sixteen. My dad wore it all his life, even when he was sick. You can still see the marks on the leather strap where he had to tighten it on his wrist when he got thinner and thinner. I ran my fingers along the grooves, thinking—one month, two months, three months—and then nothing. My throat hurt. I held the watch face to my cheek, the glass cool against my skin. Then I set it to the right time by Mom's little bedside clock, wound it up, and put it back in the box. I could still hear it ticking when I closed and locked the lid. I was really, really glad nobody had taken the watch. And I was relieved too. Because if someone *had* been in our house, that watch would have been long gone. I could relax.

The doorbell rang, making me jump. No need to be nervous anymore, for Pete's sake!

But I went in the living room and peeked through the window before I opened the door.

It was Miss Sarah. She gave me a paper plate of cookies covered with Saran wrap. "I baked these for you and your mom," she said.

"Oh thanks." I peeled off a corner and sampled one. It was still warm. "Good," I said.

"And Marcus. Tell your mother she may share them with the young man upstairs."

"He's upstairs *outside*, Miss Sarah," I said. "He's just renting our apartment. He's just our paying tenant."

Miss Sarah sniffed. "I understand he was married, once."

"That's what he said."

"He had a child, too."

"I know." Somehow I didn't like talking about Nick with Miss Sarah. It seemed disloyal, although I couldn't think why.

Miss Sarah sniffed again. "I expect he'll be eating Christmas dinner with us."

She means with Mom and me and her and Miss Coriander. Mom always invites them for Christmas dinner if we're home and not at Grandma's in Minnesota. Mom said we couldn't afford Minnesota this year. I try not to be suspicious that we could afford it OK but that she just wants to be here because of Nick.

"I expect she will ask him for dinner," I said. "I mean, he'd be all on his own." I tried to sound full of Christmas cheer. But thinking of Nick and Mom didn't make it that easy.

CHAPTER 4

I put the blackthorn stick back in the hall stand, peeled the Saran wrap off the cookies, and ate one shaped like a Christmas bell. Cookies help me think. So Miss Coriander and Miss Sarah think there is something serious between Mom and Nick. Well, they're wrong, that's all.

The jigsaw puzzle Mom and I are working on lay scattered on the big coffee table. When it's finished it will be the San Clemente Mission with its low adobe buildings and the gardens where the pigeons strut, fat and sassy. Last night I'd sifted through the pieces forever, looking for the one that had the spread of a pigeon's tail. I began looking again, but the photo of Mom kept pushing itself into the front of my brain.

The tree lights winked cheerfully on the ceiling, reflected in the dark blankness of the big window. I got up quickly and drew the drapes. There! Cozier. Safer. Usually I don't even bother closing the drapes, but now was different.

It was time to go anyway and fix dinner, which I like to do. It's interesting putting things together and coming up with something delicious.

It had taken some time for me to convince Mom that I'd be careful if she let me learn to cook, and then we'd had to go through all the possible dangers and what I'd do if they happened. Nothing had ever happened.

Tonight I made a meat loaf, and cheese muffins from a mix. I was just setting the timer when I heard Mom's car, so I grabbed the cookie plate and met her at the door between the kitchen and the garage.

"Hi, honey," she said.

"Hi. Miss Sarah sent you these."

Mom looked exhausted. I stood aside, and she slipped off her shoes and padded past me to flop in the kitchen chair. "Here." I put the biggest cookie on the plate into her hand.

Five years ago I'd heard my aunt Charlie say to Mom, "But how are you going to manage, Caroline? Going out to work every day? Having Marcus to take care of?"

I'd interrupted. "I'll take care of myself. Nobody needs to worry about me." I was eight years old at the time. They'd laughed, but I'd meant it. And I would take care of Mom, too.

Jarvis', where Mom works, is the busiest department store in the mall and the mall is loony tunes at Christmas time. Last year our class went caroling there and instead of singing "jingle bells, jingle bells," Robbie and I sang "malls of hell, malls of hell." Nobody knew the difference. I think some people even joined in.

Mom groaned and put her feet up on an empty chair. "And to think tomorrow night I have to work till eight. Will you be OK, honey?"

"Eight? Sure I'll be OK." I hadn't meant to say it so loudly, the way you do when you hope someone's going to believe you.

Mom fluffed my hair. "Eight *is* kind of late. But Nick will be up in his place if you need him." She had her elbows on the table, holding her favorite mug.

"Yeah, sure. Nick! And if he's not up there he's down here," I muttered.

Mom gave me one of her quick, questioning looks, but neither of us commented on my comment. Probably because we both knew it was true.

Nick's here tonight. Mom acted surprised when he came down, but I don't think she was. Not very. She'd saved the last four of Miss Sarah's cookies.

"You can take these two for your lunch tomorrow, Marcus," she said. The other two she put on a plate. Nick got them.

He and Mom sat poring over the jigsaw puzzle.

"Come help us, Marcus," Mom said, but I didn't want to sit there with Nick.

"Naw. I'm watching *A Christmas Carol.*" I sort of watched it. But now and then I'd glance up, keeping an eye on them.

Nick's hair gleamed yellow in the lamplight, the hair on his head, the hair on his arms. I must say Nick is the hairiest person I've ever seen. He is like a big golden bear with his twinkly eyes and great, large hands, except that he doesn't shamble along like a bear. He's fast, like a tiger on its toes. I guess Nick is about the healthiest, fittest guy in the whole world. That's probably why he teaches phys. ed.

I couldn't help noticing the way Mom had perked up since he'd come down. She really enjoys doing her jigsaws.

"Sure you don't want to help us with this?" she asked me again.

In a grumpy voice I said, "I told you already I don't."

"And Marcus Mullen is not a boy who changes his mind easily," Nick said, smiling across at me.

I sat trying to figure out if there was some hidden meaning in that remark. I often look for hidden meanings in things Nick says. Sometimes he seems to know me pretty well for someone who's just a paying tenant.

"I think I'll skip the end of the movie and hit the sack," I said, getting up and stretching. "Good night."

"Good night."

Later, I listened while Mom locked up. I heard her tiptoe past my door. I almost called her in right then to tell her I was worried about a couple of things, but I didn't. No use upsetting her.

That's what I said to Robbie the next afternoon. "What's the point in upsetting her? It's not as if the key's missing," I said. "I just goofed somehow, putting it back."

"You're sure?" Robbie asked.

"Sure I'm sure."

We were on our way to Henry's Bike Shop to see if my Campies had come in.

"Well OK, then," Robbie said.

At Henry's we headed straight through the front showroom, which was filled with parents and kids picking out bikes for Christmas. The back workroom says EMPLOYEES ONLY, but it's OK for Robbie and me to go in. Henry knows us because we mess around here so much.

The back workroom is great, with tires hanging from the walls, chrome wheels like giant mobiles dangling from the ceiling, and taken-apart bikes waiting for help on the work stands. The place smells magical, like our garage at home, only more so.

Henry was there himself.

"Hi, Hot Shot," he said to me without looking up from trueing a wheel. "They haven't come in yet."

"But Henry . . ." I began.

"I told you, Marcus. I can sell you other pedals. Cost you less than the Campagnolas, and your mom won't know the difference."

"I would know. The bike would know. Henry, that would be like having a racehorse with Clydesdale legs."

Henry grinned. "Well, you have four days yet before Christmas. Keep checking."

"I will, don't worry."

Robbie and I stopped again outside to poke around in Henry's big, green trash can. It's incredible the good stuff Henry junks. It was here that I'd found the Masi frame, all bent and buckled, the frame that was the start of Mom's Christmas present.

"Are you sure this won't fold on her, Henry?" I'd asked, squinting along the frame with one eye shut. "I don't want this bike collapsing, not to mention my mom."

"Is she planning on riding the marathon?" Henry asked.

I shook my head.

"Then it's not going to fall to pieces," he'd said.

Bit by bit I'd found everything I needed for the bike in Henry's trash can. Everything except the Campies.

Today the only thing worth taking was a mucky old piece of chain that I thought I could use sometime. I dragged it along the sidewalk behind me. Then Robbie and I tied our legs together and pretended we were on the run from a chain gang.

We came to a clanking stop at my driveway.

"Hi, Patchin," Robbie called across the street, but Patchin didn't even wag his tail. "Deaf as a dish," Robbie said, shaking his head.

I bent to unhook our chain, and when I straightened I saw that Robbie was staring at our house.

"Marcus?" he said. "You didn't hang that key back under the tree, did you?"

"Why?" I began, feeling nervous again right away. "Do you see something, Robbie?"

"I don't see a darned thing. I just wondered."

I took a deep breath. "You scared the spit out of me there." I hung the chain across my shoulders and patted the pocket of my jeans. "Don't worry. The key's safe in here. And the house is locked up tightly. No one could possibly get in."

But I was wrong about that.

CHAPTER

5

It's not hard for me to pass the time. In fact, as Mom had told Nick, I like being home alone.

After Robbie left, I worked for a while on my stamp collection and then I went out to admire Mom's bike, pedalless but still sleek and shining as a Lamborghini.

Inside the house the phone rang.

It was Robbie.

"Everything OK?" he asked.

"Sure everything's OK."

"Well it may not be for long. I just saw Anjelica Trotter and she was on her bike, heading in the direction of your house."

"*My* house?"

"Your street, anyway. She was turning your corner."

"You're kidding!" I stared around the kitchen as if somehow Anjelica might have snuck in and hidden herself under the table. "But why?" I asked. "How long ago did you see her?"

"About two minutes. She ought to be just about riding up your front drive now."

"Oh criminy!" The panic was back, full gale force. "She wouldn't come here, would she, Robbie? I mean, I didn't forget any of my books and school's out and—"

"You should let her in if she comes," Robbie said. "*I* would."

"I bet you wouldn't. What would you talk to her about?"

"I'd think of something. I'd ask how come her top grew so much."

"Ha!" I said. "You're such a liar. Anyway, it's too late for her to come. It's—"

"What do you mean late? It's only twenty after four."

"That's all? Man! I thought . . ." Twenty after four was a long way from eight.

The doorbell rang.

I swear I could hear Robbie breathing.

"It's her," he said. "Let her in. Call me

back. Maybe she has the mistletoe." He hung up the phone.

"Robbie?" I begged, but he was gone.

Now I could hear *me* breathing.

I tiptoed into the living room and pulled back a corner of the drape. If Anjelica was out there, I hoped she wouldn't see the drape move, because I was just going to pretend there was no one home.

Nick stood on the porch in his khaki shorts and red Cougar sweatshirt. I was so glad to see him I even smiled and said, "Hi," when I opened the door.

He looked surprised, but he smiled back right away.

"Where's your key?" I asked, remembering quickly that he and I are definitely not close buddies.

"I knew you were here," Nick said. "You don't think I'd just walk in on you, do you? I mean, a guy needs his privacy." His eyes still smiled at me, real friendly. "Anyway, I've ordered a pizza to be delivered for six o'clock, extra large, no anchovies. You want to come up and help me eat it?"

What was this? Be nice to Caroline's boy?

"Thanks," I said, "but I have leftovers that I have to use. Good leftovers," I added. It really bugged me that he knew I hate anchovies. Mom must have told him that, along with everything else. Talk about a guy's privacy! Or he just guessed. Maybe everybody in the world hates anchovies.

"Whatever." Nick didn't seem disappointed. "I'm going to cut the grass now, so it will look good for Christmas."

"OK. I'll open the garage door for you."

I went back into the house and through to the garage, and pushed the wall button that lifts the heavy door. The center light came on automatically too, the way it does.

I watched while Nick wheeled out the mower, filled the tank with gas, and started the motor. I really couldn't understand why I suddenly had the urge to grab a rake and go work with him. If he were my Dad that's what I'd do. It would be nice, cutting the grass in neat little stripes, stopping to horse around a bit, throw grass at each other, stuff like that.

I dropped the sheet over Mom's bike and left the door open so Nick could put the mower back when he finished.

That wasn't till after six.

The pizza van came and I saw Nick take the big, white box and run up the stairs and back down with money for the delivery guy. I watched him put the mower away and heard the door hiss closed.

I took the meat loaf from the fridge. It seemed to have shrunk. Had we really eaten so much last night? Robbie says in his house things shrink overnight because his dad likes to sneak out of bed for a midnight snack. Mom doesn't do that. I don't either. I was still staring at the meat loaf when the phone rang.

"Is Anjelica still there?" Robbie whispered.

"She didn't come."

"Shoot! I thought you'd have great things to tell me."

"Yeah, sure," I said sarcastically.

"You sound in a great mood," Robbie said. "You're disappointed, that's what. You're bummed out because you *like* Anjelica Trotter and she didn't come."

"I am *not*!"

He was still saying "Anjelica Trotter, Anjelica Trotter" as I banged down the phone.

Grief! It was seven o'clock. Pretty soon

Mom would be home and I'd been OK, not nervous about being alone or anything. Big deal. Well, it was a big deal, considering the missing-key thing. Of course Nick had been outside just about the whole time. Did he and Mom arrange that? Had he told her about yesterday and how he'd had to search the house because I thought I heard something? And then, last night, had he told Mom, "Don't worry, Caroline. I'll be right there outside, where he can see me"?

Naw. Mom would know I'd hate that.

I waited to eat till she came home, and then we watched TV for a while and went to bed early. If Mom noticed that I took the blackthorn stick with me, she didn't say.

Something wakened me in the night. I didn't think it was a noise because I can sleep through anything. I even slept through one of our earthquakes once, or I would have if Dad hadn't scooped me up. I remember everything tilting around us and the way he'd staggered and that I'd laughed.

I lay in bed wondering what could have wakened me now. It must have been a dream. I couldn't remember dreaming, but my heart was suddenly doing that loud, bumpy thing again.

I sat up and listened to the silence. Nothing. My room wasn't that dark and I could see all its comfortable, familiar outlines. I knew I should get up and check around the house. But I didn't want to. I should at least look in Mom's room and make sure she was OK.

I reached under the bed for the stick and went barefoot from my room. Mom sleeps with her door slightly open. I pushed it wider and peered in. Her miniblinds were half raised, the window partway open. It's fixed so the opening's too small for anyone to take off the screen and crawl in. By the paleness of moonlight I could see her in the bed, the dark spread of her hair across the pillow.

I checked the front door. It was locked, with the chain safely in place. The back door to the garage was locked. The stick felt good, heavy and knobby in my hand, as I switched on lights and went room to room. Nobody there. Except for Mom and me, the house was empty.

I went back to bed and tried to remember what dream I'd had that had woken me up and set me off like that. My feet were so cold that I had to get back out and grab some socks and put them on to warm up. Sometime later, still listening, I fell asleep.

The patter of Mom's shower woke me up in the morning, and by the time I'd yawned my way into the kitchen she had coffee made and was dressed for work.

"I meant to be up early," I said, rubbing my eyes. "I meant to fix your breakfast."

Mom dropped a kiss on the top of my head.

"I heard you in the bathroom last night," she said.

"Yeah. I was up," I said uneasily. If I told her about that night prowling, she'd be sure to have me go next door today or, heaven forbid, arrange something with our famous paying tenant.

"Don't forget we have a date tonight," she said. "You're meeting me after work."

"Are you kidding? I wouldn't forget."

"What else are you doing, Marcus?"

"Robbie and I are going along Lake Avenue. It's the Merchants' Christmas Fair with all those free cookies and punch and stuff."

"Good. And if you need anything, you can run next door." For a minute I thought she *was* going to add "or up to Nick's," but our eyes met and she didn't add anything.

After she left I sat thinking. It was funny that she'd heard me last night when I'd been so quiet. And that she'd thought she heard me in the bathroom when I hadn't been in the bathroom at all. . . .

CHAPTER 6

I called Henry's Bike Shop just before I went out to wait for Robbie, but Mom's darn Campies hadn't come in yet. I was glad I wasn't going to be hanging around the house all day alone worrying about them—and other things. Robbie's a good person to be with if you don't want to worry.

He and I walked along Lake Avenue in the sunshine, sampling the free this and the free that. Free popcorn in little paper pokes. Free candy canes. Free mulled cider from what the lady in the long frilly dress called the wassail bowl.

"You boys aren't driving, are you?" the lady asked, acting as though she thought we might have been. When we told her no, she filled our glasses a second time. "I'm only kidding," she said. "There's no alcohol in this." She took a glass for herself. "It's awfully hot for this dress."

"You look very nice though," Robbie said, super politely. Robbie is real smooth, and I could tell the lady was pleased.

"Why thank you, young man," she said, filling our glasses a third time.

We moseyed on.

There was a Santa Claus in front of just about every shop, and there were carolers in ski caps and scarves and mittens, carrying lighted red candles in candlesticks.

"Hey look!" I gave Robbie a dig. "It's the Pacific High School chorus! The ones who sang at school."

We squirmed to the front of the small crowd and wiggled our fingers at the chorus in a friendly way. They were finishing the last jolly line of "Rudolph the Red-Nosed Reindeer," the one that tells how Rudolph will go down in history, and were starting to straggle on to their next stop when Robbie tugged on the arm of one of the guys. He was wearing a red-and-white scarf, so long you could have used it to lasso mustangs. It was the singer with the mustache, the one who'd been in the front line of the chorus.

"Remember us?" Robbie asked. "You sang in our cafetorium."

"Yeah, sure." The guy stared at us blankly. Then he grinned and pointed at me with his mittened fingers. "I remember *you.* You were sitting next to the girl with the blond hair. Kind of well built, for junior high. You know the one?"

"Anjelica Trotter," Robbie said.

The guy curled his tongue up around his mustache, I guess to check if it was still there. "Anjelica Trotter! Well! By the way, I'm Fred Garcia."

"Hi, Fred," Robbie said.

I didn't say anything.

"You don't happen to have this Anjelica Trotter's phone number?"

Fred was asking me and I was staring at him as if I didn't understand English.

He bent toward us and candle wax splashed on the sidewalk. His forehead was beaded with sweat. "Confidentially," he said, "I happened to notice that she had a very intriguing message printed on the spine of her notebook."

"I love somebody," Robbie said helpfully. Robbie is a very helpful person.

"Yeah. Pity she didn't think to put her phone number on her notebook too. I'd have asked for it, but this big hunk of a teacher was standing right there. You don't happen to know her number, offhand, yourselves?" he asked.

"Marcus?" Robbie turned to me, his eyes big and innocent. I felt like punching him out. I felt like punching them both out.

"I *don't* happen to know it," I said. "And if I *did* happen to know it I wouldn't happen to give it to just anybody on the street who asked for it."

"Quite right. Here, hold this." Fred shoved the dripping candle into my hand and bit off one of his mittens. He used it to wipe his forehead, then fished in his pocket and came up with an old envelope. "It's warm," he said, and began searching his pocket again.

"You need a pencil?" Robbie offered him one shaped like a candy cane that we'd just been given free at Tilton Hardware. Robbie is so helpful he makes me want to throw up.

One of the carolers called, "Come on, Fred."

"I'll be right with you," Fred said.

He wrote quickly and shoved the envelope at me. "My phone number," he said. "Why don't you ask Anjelica to give me a call?" He grabbed the candle and was gone, the end of his scarf trailing behind him. I stepped on it so fast, it came off and he had to turn back to scoop it up. He dropped his candle.

By this time half the chorus was yelling at him.

"Jerk!" I said, when he finally got everything together. I shoved the envelope with his phone number into one of the wire trash baskets that hung from the light pole. "That guy's old enough to be Anjelica's father."

"*I* think Anjelica might like a mature guy like Fred," Robbie said. "For her red-and-green 'Color Me Christmas' lipstick. And her new top."

He was walking backward in front of me, talking and grinning. "How come you're not giving her Fred's phone number? That wasn't very nice of you, throwing it away, Marcus. You know why you did it, don't you?"

"You look really stupid walking backward," I told him coldly. I was ready to start a giant-sized row, but just then a lady with a tray offered us little crackers with cheese on them. The food calmed us down, and by the time we'd eaten our way to the corner of Lake and Cordova, we were OK again.

The clock on the Bank of America building said four fifteen.

"I'm going to be late for Mom," I told Robbie. "I still have to go home and pick up the two Wish Tree packages to bring to the mall. Let's move."

We walked fast along Cordova, finishing the crackers and cheese we'd stashed in our pockets.

"I like that Wish Tree thing you and your mom do," Robbie said. "It's neat. We should start that in my family."

"I like it too."

Robbie munched a handful of broken crackers. "Why didn't we bum a couple of extra drinks? These things are dry."

"We have lemonade at home," I told him. "But you'll have to be quick."

As soon as we got to our house, I noticed that Nick's car wasn't there. Across the street Patchin drowsed in the afternoon sun, and

Miss Sarah was in her driveway next door, washing her car. It's a big old black Buick, shaped like a humpback whale, and she's all the time hosing it off and waxing it, although it doesn't go many places. On Sundays its open trunk is filled with the flowers that she and Miss Coriander take to their church. Then it's like some strange funeral car going slowly and solemnly down the street.

"Good afternoon, Miss Sarah," Robbie said. "You're looking very well."

Miss Sarah sniffed. "Good afternoon, Robert. Marcus! You'd better hurry or you'll be late for your mother." She twisted the hose nozzle to "spray" so it would be less noisy. "The Rabbit Hutch in the mall has a special today. I saw it in the *Star News.* Turkey salad. I'd have thought they'd have turkey salad after Christmas, but it's not good to eat it then. They take the leftover turkey off people's plates and mince it up. But before Christmas should be safe."

"Oh. Well. I'll tell Mom and we can check it out. Thanks, Miss Sarah." Yuk, I thought.

I can never understand how Miss Sarah knows everything that's going on. She's like one of those Greek oracles. I wondered if she knew about Nick's photograph of Mom. I wondered if she knew when it was taken. There was no way to ask. I took my key from my pocket, dusted the crumbs off it, and unlocked our door.

The living room was empty and tidy, the tree lights off. The jigsaw puzzle was a blob of color on the coffee table beside the two wrapped Wish Tree gifts. Everything just the way I'd left it. What other way would it be?

"You want lemonade too?" Robbie asked me, heading for the kitchen.

I followed. "Naw. I'm OK."

In the kitchen the wall clock lurched as it came to the half hour. It always lurches on the half and the whole. The faucet dripped gently into the morning cereal dish I'd left in the sink. The loaf of bread I'd taken from the freezer sat, defrosting. I eased off my backpack and slid it on the table.

"What's that smell?" Robbie had his head up, sniffing around. "Do you smell something?"

"What kind of something?" I sniffed and smelled it too.

"Peanut butter," Robbie said triumphantly. He slopped the lemonade pitcher onto the table beside my backpack and got himself a glass. "I have a nose for peanut butter. You had peanut butter for breakfast, right? You had a lot, if the smell's still in the air."

I opened the cupboard and looked at the jar that sat where it always sat.

"I haven't touched this in days," I said.

"Well, somebody has," Robbie said.

"What do you mean, *somebody*?" I couldn't figure why the least little word made me nervous now. Ever since the key. My brain kept telling me that there was nothing to be nervous about, but the rest of me wasn't getting the message. I tiptoed across to where the loaf was defrosting.

"Why are you walking like that?" Robbie asked.

"Sh!" One end of the loaf didn't look quite right. Had the wax-paper wrapping been opened very carefully? Had bread been taken from the end and then had someone closed it again, folding the wrapping exactly the same way? There was a gap with just air where three or four slices of bread should have been. I tried to remember if it had been tightly closed this morning. Sometimes Mom and I do take a few pieces for toast or something before we freeze a loaf. That could be it. Or maybe Nick had come in and borrowed some. Then he'd fixed himself a couple of peanut butter sandwiches. Want to bet he'd helped himself yesterday to that meat loaf too? No wonder things were shrinking. Go right ahead, make yourself at home, Nick, I thought bitterly.

"Is everything OK?" Robbie sounded semi-nervous himself. I guess it's catching.

"Sure." I threw the bread in the bread drawer.

"Good. For a minute there you were acting weird."

"Hurry up," I said. "I'm in a rush, you know."

Robbie drained the last of the lemonade and burped. Robbie may be smooth at times but he has the worst, wettest burp in the world. I pushed him ahead of me into the living room, grabbed the packages, and took a last look around.

He watched as I double-locked the front door.

"That was quick," Miss Sarah called over the hedge.

"I know." I slid the key in my pocket. "Did you notice what time Nick left today, Miss Sarah?"

"Nick? Oh, you mean your mother's friend?" Before I could protest, she said, "He left right after you did. He drives that car of his altogether too fast in the driveway."

"Did he just come down the steps, get in the car, and take off?"

Miss Sarah released the trigger on the end of the hose to stop the water entirely so that there was no noise and she could concentrate on this new development, whatever it was.

"What else would you expect him to do, Marcus?"

"Nothing. He didn't come back?"

"No. Why, Marcus?" Her nose twitched. Miss Sarah has a rather long nose. When I was little I'd asked Mom if that was why she sniffed so much, and Mom said no, and I must never, ever ask her that.

"I'd like to know why you have all these questions about that young man, Marcus," she said.

"No reason. 'Bye, Miss Sarah."

"That Nick's getting out of hand coming in your house like that," Robbie said as we walked down the driveway. "He's taking stuff, isn't he?" I nodded. "You should tell your mom."

"I'm going to."

We parted on the sidewalk, me going east, Robbie west.

I walked as quickly as I could. Of course it was Nick, and I *should* tell Mom. Paying tenants have no business taking over like that. Imagine him, coming in and— I slowed. But when did he come in? My stomach was fluttering. It had to be Nick. Who else could it be?

CHAPTER 7

I was ten minutes late for Mom. As I came up on the escalator, I saw her standing in front of the Rabbit Hutch and for a minute she wasn't my mom at all. She was just a lady, and I saw her the way any of the people pushing past would see her. Thin, not very tall, loose dark hair, wearing a gray skirt and a gray-and-pink-striped blouse that was tied at the neck. *Pretty.* Young-looking. Sad. The way Nick had seen her the day he took that picture. Oh, Mom. Don't be sad. It's OK.

I was at the top now. She noticed me and waved and the sadness was gone.

She pointed to a round Santa Claus, asleep on his back on one of the mall benches. He was snoring gently, and on the mound of his stomach a printed notice moved up and down as he puffed in and out. It said: "Don't wake me till Christmas Eve. I'm resting up for the big night."

A bunch of little kids stood staring at him, mouths open. Mom put her arm around my shoulders and hugged me tight against her for just a minute. "I was thinking what a pity it is that Santa has to end for kids." Was that truly what she'd been thinking? Why she'd looked sad?

"Only three days till Christmas," she said. "I'm beginning to feel like Scrooge, wishing it were all over. That's what working at Jarvis' Department Store will do to you."

This didn't seem the right time to bring up Nick, but maybe there would never be a right time, and I had to get it out.

"Mom? I have to tell you something. I think Nick's coming into our house when we're not there."

Mom's face seemed to soften. "Oh honey, what if he is? Do you mind that much? I gave him a key for emergencies, like the time I left the iron on and—"

"And so he can go in and use the washer and dryer. I know. He told me. Anyway, Miss

Coriander and Miss Sarah have an emergency key."

"That's true." Mom bit her lip. "I'm not sure he does come in when we're not there. Nick's pretty sensitive . . ."

"Sure," I muttered. She didn't seem to hear.

". . . but if it bothers you to think he *might*, well, I'll just tell him not to."

"I think he eats our food."

"Our food?" I heard Mom's astonishment, the whine in my own voice.

"Well, I can't imagine why he'd do that," she said after a pause. "What makes you think he does?"

"I think he took a piece of the meat loaf, and he definitely ate bread, and used the peanut butter . . ." I stopped. "Forget it," I said. "I'm not even sure. I just thought you'd want to know."

"I do want to know. You were right to tell me, Marcus. I'll ask him first—"

"No. Don't. I feel dumb now. It'll only make me look stupid, and I hate looking stupid in front of him."

Mom nodded seriously, her eyes on my face. Then for some reason she hugged me again. "So?" she said. "You remembered to go home first and get the gifts. Shall we go to the Wish Tree before we eat?"

"Let's. That will give me a chance to get hungrier. Robbie and I ate a bunch of stuff earlier." She took one of the packages from me as we walked through the mall, and I could see that the subject of Nick was finished, for now anyway.

The Wish Tree started three or four years ago. At the beginning of December it's hung with Christmas ornaments made of paper, each with a wish written on it, signed by a foster child. There were 800 wishes on the tree to begin with, and they'd all been taken by people who wanted to make a wish come true for one of the kids.

The wish I'd taken was for Eric G, age nine. He wanted a Clue game, and I'd bought it with my own money and wrapped it in Christmas paper that had rocket ships and space Santas on it. I was glad I'd taken Eric's wish. He wasn't that much younger than I was, and he didn't have a dad *or* a mom. "Remember how you used to like Clue yourself?" Mom had asked.

"Yeah." Maybe I still did. Maybe that was

what I'd been doing these past couple of days—playing a big, old game of Clue. I put the flat package with Eric's name on it in the gift collection barrel.

The wish Mom had taken was for Abby M, age two, who wanted a baby doll. We'd gotten her a really nice one in Jarvis' toy department at 20 percent off, Mom's employee discount. The doll had a pink dress and drank from a baby bottle. Mom had held it for the longest time before she wrapped it, and I thought that she could be thinking how she might have had a little girl herself, if Dad hadn't been sick for so long, hadn't died. Maybe she would have been buying *her* a doll this Christmas. There were a lot of things that might have been different for Mom. I thought she'd been weepy when she was wrapping Abby M's gift, but now she looked happy as she put it into the barrel. "Merry Christmas, Abby," she whispered. And then she said to me, "Isn't it nice to be able to make children's Christmas wishes come true, even just a little bit?"

One of the volunteers smiled her thanks at us, and Mom and I stood for a minute in this quiet little corner with the mall crowds bustling past us, the two of us like an island in a river. The tree made me think of far-off forests and clean mountain air. Christmas music splashed in little bursts around us. "This is one of my favorite parts of Christmas," Mom said. "It helps me to remember what it's all about." She took my hand and held it all the way to the Rabbit Hutch. I didn't mind.

I guess I had made the wrong choice, though, in going to the Wish Tree first, because now there was a line to get into the restaurant. While we stood there I gave Mom Miss Sarah's message about the turkey salad, and then I noticed that Mom was smiling and nodding at someone in the line in front of us.

"Marcus!" she whispered. "Quick, what are their names? You know, the parents of that girl in your class?"

I stepped out of line to look and was face to face with Anjelica Trotter. I don't know which one of us was more shocked. *I* was flabbergasted. Not because she was here. Half of the world is in this mall before Christmas, and half of the shoppers want to eat at the Rabbit Hutch. It was because of the way Anjelica looked!

"What's her name?" Mom asked softly, and

I got a grip on myself and said, "Anjelica Trotter."

"Right. I remember." And then Mom was saying, "Nice to meet you again Mrs. Trotter, Mr. Trotter. Hello, Anjelica."

She and Anjelica's parents were smiling at each other. I was staring at Anjelica. She was staring at her feet.

Mr. and Mrs. Trotter were having a whispered conversation, and then they left their place in the line, let the people between us go ahead of them, and stepped back so they were next to us. Anjelica trailed behind.

"You know my son, Marcus?" Mom asked, and Anjelica's parents said, "Yes, yes," and then her father said, "You are the young man who had the excellent stamp collection in the open house way back in fifth grade."

I was mumbling yes and making myself concentrate on him and not Anjelica, and Mom was beaming and saying, "How nice of you to remember." I was looking so intently at Anjelica's father that I could probably have gone home and drawn such a good picture of him that anybody would instantly pick him out of a police lineup, not that he's ever likely to be in one. Small, a little chubby, glasses. And her mother. Brownish hair, small. Very serious-looking but nice, homey. My eyes kept popping toward Anjelica.

Anjelica's face was bare, the way it used to be. She had only one set of eyebrows. Her lips were pale pink instead of red and green, her hair was pretty and soft, and under her yellow sweater her top was totally flat. Not totally flat. Not like mine. But it was normal-looking. I couldn't get over it. Anjelica looked the way she'd looked in sixth grade. Anjelica was absolutely gorgeous.

"I expect you and Anjelica know each other quite well." Her mother smiled across at me.

"Oh, ah, yes." I was overcome. Overcome by Anjelica.

Mom was talking now about Christmas and how busy she was at work, while Anjelica and I both gazed into space. I was wondering if she could have a twin sister. Like the good and the bad, or the shy and the pushy. But Mrs. Trotter had called her Anjelica. You wouldn't call twin sisters the same name!

This silence between us was getting embarrassing.

"Uh, how's it going, Anjelica?" I had to push the words out.

"All right." Her eyelashes were soft and stubby like the bristles on a horsehair paint-brush.

The line started to move, and we shuffled with it.

"It was nice of you to bring over my book that day," I said desperately. "I really appreciated it."

"That's OK. I go by your house all the time." She stopped and gave a little gulp.

"You go by *my* house? What for?"

"I mean . . . not often. I mean, not really." Anjelica looked as if she might cry.

"Next please," the Rabbit Hutch hostess called. "I can take seven." She began counting and touching shoulders, and the Trotters trotted off, wishing us a Merry Christmas and saying how nice it had been to see us again. Anjelica gave me a last mournful glance.

"Anjelica seems like a nice girl," Mom said when they'd gone. "She's quite shy, isn't she?"

Criminy! Mom ought to hear her in school and see her too. Talk about a switcheroo. Fortunately I didn't have to give my opinion, because the hostess appeared again and pointed us to a seat by the window. I guess at this time of year the hostess doesn't bother to escort you.

Mom and I ordered steaks and french fries, despite Miss Sarah's turkey salad recommendation. We didn't talk about Nick at all. I admit I stretched my neck hoping for another glimpse of Anjelica, but she'd vanished into a dark corner of the Rabbit Hutch. I couldn't even see her when Mom and I were on the way out.

We stopped at Grandma's Bake Shop to get oatmeal muffins to eat in the car. In a basket on the counter were cookies, big as dinner plates, wrapped in plastic and tied with red ribbon.

"Oh, look! Butterscotch. Nick's favorite," Mom said, then bit her lip and glanced down at me.

"It's OK, Mom. You don't have to never mention his name, just because I don't like him that much."

"I'm sorry you don't like him, Marcus," Mom said in a way that made my heart beat fast with worry. "He likes you."

"I'm sure." My horrible surly voice was

back, and I tried to make things better by saying: "Get him some of the cookies if you want. I don't care." That didn't make it any better. I sounded surlier and meaner than ever, and Mom's mouth tightened.

"I think I will," she said.

The Grandma's Bake Shop lady asked which kind we wanted, peanut butter or butterscotch.

"Butterscotch," Mom said. "He doesn't like peanut butter."

"He doesn't?" I asked, and Mom gave me a sideways glance as if to say: "See? And you were accusing him. Did you think he ate our peanut butter?" Well, maybe she'd gotten it wrong. Or maybe he just didn't like it in cookies. I knew what I knew.

The lady put the two big cookies in a bag, and I offered to carry them, but Mom said, no, they weren't heavy. I hated Nick even more for spoiling our night. It's weird how that guy's always around, even when he's not invited.

We drove home through lighted streets, bright with bells and prancing plastic reindeer. A group of Hare Krishnas in long white robes rang silver bells on the corner. They looked like Christmas angels except they had no wings or hair. There were carolers out still, but they weren't the ones from Pacific High School. Would Anjelica have liked that message from Fred Garcia, the one I'd thrown in the trash? She hadn't been so mature tonight. Fred wouldn't have liked her tonight. I wondered how much Mom liked Nick. I wondered why he was doing the things he was doing.

The light was on in his apartment. Mom parked our car behind his and leaned into the backseat for the cookie bag. "I guess I'll give him these tomorrow," she said.

"Why not now?" I asked. "Then you could see him. And an evening without Nick is such a waste of time."

Mom pushed back her hair. "Did you know you're getting to be rude, Marcus?"

"You mean because I don't like Nick?"

"No. Because you never miss a chance to be horrible about him. And he doesn't deserve it."

She opened her car door. "Since you suggested it, I think I will run up and give him these now. They'll be fresher." She hesitated.

"I don't suppose you want to come?"

I stepped out of the car before I answered. The night was cool and the sky bright with stars. From the direction of the Clarks' house came the smell of something sweet and spicy. I glanced up at Nick's apartment. Actually, I didn't want Mom going up there by herself, the two of them maybe talking about me. Mom: "He's getting so rude and impossible, I don't know what I'm going to do with him." Nick: "It's hard for the boy, Caroline. He'll get over it." Why did I know Nick would be reasonable and, in a way, on my side? Why couldn't he be rotten about me so Mom would start not liking him?

Our house looked dark and somehow mysterious. I didn't really want to go into it by myself. "I guess I'll come with you," I said.

"Good!" I saw the glimmer of Mom's smile in the half dark, heard the pleasure in her voice. She put her arms around my shoulders. "Let's go."

I tagged behind her as she climbed the wooden steps to Nick's, her heels tapping out a happy little rhythm. I sneaked a couple of glances at our house below. Why hadn't I left a lamp on in the porch or living room? A car passed on the street, and its headlights gleamed on the blankness of a window. For a second I thought I saw movement behind there. But it was only the tree branches or the top of the oleander hedge reflected in the trail of light. It was nothing at all. I hurried to catch up with Mom.

CHAPTER 8

I guess Nick had heard us coming, because he had his door open and his outside light on before we got there. "Hi," he said. Boy, did he look happy to see us! A great, big, happy, old bear.

Mom gave him the bag and said, "Cookies! For your sweet tooth." He peered inside and said, "Caroline! Thank you!"

I swear, he couldn't have sounded more grateful if she'd given him a Porsche or a Ferrari. In my opinion, he overdid it a bit.

"Marcus thought we should bring them up to you tonight," Mom said, and Nick smiled at me. "Thanks Marcus. These are great. Come in, both of you. Sit down! Marcus, try the wicker chair. It's pretty good. Caroline, you sit here."

When had this Caroline business started? I thought she was supposed to be Mrs. Mullen to him. I guess when you're poring over a jigsaw puzzle night after night it's pretty hard to say, "Hey, Mrs. Mullen, I've found this piece of sky," or "Yes, I will have a cup of coffee, Mrs. Mullen. And I'll take a butterscotch cookie if you happen to have one. They're my favorites." Caroline *would* be more natural.

The wicker chair creaked but he was right, it was comfortable. Nick made us hot chocolate. He had one Santa mug, which he gave me. Mom said, "I'm getting fat and sassy and it isn't even Christmas yet."

"You're not fat," Nick said. "You will never be fat."

That sounded like a pretty familiar remark for him to make to my mother. It was the kind of smirky, just-for-laughs thing Robbie would say. But Nick wasn't being smirky. This was real, like the time I'd heard him tell her she was a beautiful woman.

I stared around the apartment. There was the bird picture I'd seen yesterday, and other photographs of birds in flight, big flocks of them taking off into a sunset sky. There was one of a nest with babies in it. They had feathers that stuck up on the tops of their heads the way Anjelica Trotter's school hair did. Mom's picture wasn't anywhere in sight.

"I guess you like birds, Nick," I said. "You must like taking pictures, period." I didn't add, "For instance, how about that one of Mom," but I tried to put a lot of extra meaning into what I did say.

Nick smiled. "I do. I teach photography as well as phys. ed., you know."

"You didn't know that, Marcus?" Mom took a sip of her hot chocolate.

"No." Obviously *she* did.

"Photography's pretty neat," Nick said. "I have an extra camera, brand-new. I bought it for my son, but . . ." He stopped. "You could borrow it if you like, Marcus. I'd be happy to give you some pointers."

What was he trying for now? A replacement son?

"No way," I said.

"Marcus!" Mom sat straight.

"I just meant that I don't want to borrow a camera, that's all," I began. "I've got so many things going right now."

"It's all right, Caroline," Nick said. "Marcus knows what he wants and what he doesn't want."

There he goes again, I thought. Taking my side.

Nick had broken the cookies into quarters. He offered the plate to me and I took a piece and said, "Thanks, Nick," so I'd come over a little more polite and Mom would be pleased. She and Nick were talking comfortably together, like friends who'd known each other for a long time. Good friends.

After a while Mom stretched and yawned. "All I need now is a hot bath and early to bed. Tomorrow's going to be hectic." She stood up. "Ready, Marcus?"

I was ready all right.

Nick walked us to the door.

"Caroline," he said, "why don't you go on? I want to speak to Marcus for a few minutes."

Uh-oh. I had a feeling this was going to be some kind of showdown. Maybe a let's-try-to-get-along-for-your-mother's-sake lecture.

"Is it a Christmas secret?" Mom had that hopeful look. "The air's filled with secrets at this time of year." She gave me a smile. "I'll see you later down at the house then, Marky."

The shadow on the window slid across my mind, even though I knew it was only the tree. "We'd better go together, Mom. I'm pretty pooped too. Can whatever it is wait till tomorrow, Nick?"

"Sure. And Marcus. Don't wait for an invitation. Come up anytime."

He called good night from the top of the stairs and stood there, letting his apartment light shine down on us. Next door I could see Miss Coriander in her kitchen stirring something in a blue bowl. Their kitchen is like a storage room, piled high with cardboard containers overflowing with the dried pods and buttons and pinecones and wire that she and Miss Sarah use to make the Christmas wreaths they give away. The Raggedy Anns Miss Sarah is making for their church sale sat in a row on the table. I could see the stacks of newspaper they keep for recycling. It looked nice. Safe and messy and normal.

Mom had taken her keys from her purse, and waved back to Nick as she opened our door.

I stepped in front of her and turned on the hall light. Nobody. Of course not. I had to quit this imagining. When I plugged in the tree, the red, blue, and yellow bulbs twinkled and shone, tumbling their colors across the ceiling. Cheerful, Christmasy. Nothing to worry about. I went around then, lighting up the whole house.

Mom met me in the hallway. "Hon, I'm going to go straight in for my bath and bed. Do you want to watch TV for a while? Or read?"

I nodded.

"I'll try not to wake you in the morning when I leave. I should be home shortly after six." She hesitated, and I thought she was going to hassle me about being rude to Nick, but instead she put her hands on my shoulders and said: "I love you very much, Marcus. Nothing can change that. Nobody can change that." She was looking so deeply into my eyes that I thought she might be able to see through them, into my brain, see the thoughts scuttling nervously around. "I truly don't know if Nick and I care for each other in any serious way," she said, "but I promise you something. I will tell you if it gets to be like that. You will be the first to know. OK?"

I tried to smile. "OK."

"Good night, Marky."

"Sleep tight, Mom."

I went back in the living room and slumped on the couch. She didn't know if she and Nick cared for each other seriously. It could all fall through. I would start thinking negatively that it would. I imagined Nick giving up the apartment, disappearing. A nice young couple with two kids would rent the place and they'd have me baby-sit and the kids would call me Unky Marky. Two kids might be too much. OK, one kid. I wondered if Anjelica Trotter had baby-sitting jobs. A lot of the girls did.

Mom was still in the bathroom, so I went through the kitchen to use the little half bath off the laundry room. On the floor, right in front of the toilet, were two clumps of bright, fresh green. My heart began pumping up a storm as I leaned over and touched one with the tip of my finger. It fell apart into a scatter of grass. What the . . . ? The other clump was still intact.

I sat back on my heels, looking at it. Nick had cut our front lawn yesterday. Somebody had walked across it since then and the grass had stuck on the soles of his shoes. The someone had come in here and used the toilet and the grass had fallen off. Who? Not Robbie or I today. Not Mom. She always drives straight into the garage. And tonight we hadn't gone near the lawn. Nick again? When? I'd watched him yesterday as he put everything away. He hadn't come in the house. Today then. But why would he come down here when he had his own bathroom upstairs? It didn't make sense. And Miss Sarah hadn't seen him. Hard for him to slip past her.

Carefully I picked up the wad of grass and cradled it in my hand. No clues here. No wonderful, distinctive rubber sole marks. Nothing. It cracked in two as I examined it and I dropped half into the toilet and flushed it away. The other piece was thicker, rubbery. I set it, whole, on the windowsill.

"Marcus?" That was Mom calling.

"Coming."

Mom was standing in the living room. She wore her dark-blue robe and her hair hung in little wet strands on her shoulders. "Have you seen my clock, Marcus?" she asked.

"Your clock? You mean your little bedside clock?"

"Yes. It's the darndest thing. I can't find it anywhere. I know it was there this morning. The alarm woke me up. Did you borrow it?"

I shook my head, feeling cold and anxious. Too many weird things going on.

"I didn't think you did. Well, how could it vanish like this?"

"Nick took it?" I hadn't meant it to be a question, but that's how it came out. Mom's face changed. I wanted to look away because I could see she was getting angry.

"I'm really tired of all this talk about Nick, Marcus. Now you're being ridiculous."

"No I'm not. He did take it. And he *is* coming in our house when he knows we're not here. Yesterday, or today, he used the toilet in our laundry room."

Mom sighed in an exasperated way. "So what if he did? Maybe he didn't want to bother going upstairs when he was in the garage, or out in the yard. That's such a big deal?"

"I just . . ." How to explain this feeling? "He came in secretly. Even Miss Sarah didn't see him."

"You mean you asked her? Honestly, Marcus! Well, it obviously *is* a big deal to you so let's just find out what Nick has to say. That would seem to be the easiest thing. We'll simply ask him if he took the clock, used the toilet, took—" She stopped. "What else is it he's supposed to have taken?"

"Bread and peanut butter," I said weakly.

"Oh yes. And the meat loaf. Didn't you mention meat loaf?"

She walked across to the phone, dialed.

"I think maybe I'm wrong," I said desperately. "Why don't we just forget it tonight? We can—"

"Nick?" Mom said into the phone. "This is Caroline. I wonder if you could come down here for a few minutes. Marcus and I would like to talk to you about something."

There was a pause before she said, "Thanks, Nick," and hung up the phone.

I guess Nick was coming.

CHAPTER 9

It must have taken Nick about a minute to run down but it seemed longer. Mom and I waited in the living room, me with my hands in my pockets. The only thing I said was: "Want me to get you a towel to dry your hair?" and she shook her head.

When he tapped the window, Mom opened the door.

"Is something wrong?" He stepped past her, looking at me.

"Sort of," I said.

"Let's go into the kitchen." Mom led the way and Nick spread his hands in a "what's up?" kind of gesture at me. He was wearing blue pajama bottoms and a short terry robe. I looked through him as if he wasn't there.

Mom and I sat at one side of the table, Nick at the other. The accused! I thought.

"Marcus is upset because he thinks you're coming here when we're not around," Mom said. "Secretly."

"What makes you think that, Marcus?" Nick asked. I wondered if it meant he was guilty because he didn't deny anything straight off.

"Because someone's been here a bunch of times. And you have a key," I said.

"Marcus thinks you're taking stuff," Mom added.

Nick folded his big hands on the table in front of him.

"I have never done that, Marcus," he said. "I *have* been here a couple of times on my own. Once because your mother asked me to let the plumber in and stay while he worked. And once . . ." He turned to Mom. "Didn't I take a delivery of something, Caroline?"

"The chair. From Krenwinkle's."

"But I didn't come secretly, and I promise I didn't take anything. I think I made myself a cup of instant coffee—"

"Oh stop it, Nick," Mom said wearily. "Marcus, can't you see how silly this is?"

I got up and took the spatula from the kitchen drawer.

"What are you doing now?" Mom asked,

but I didn't reply. I brought back the clump of grass and slid it onto the table.

Nick touched it the way I'd done.

"It was on the floor in front of the laundry-room toilet," I said.

"Not from your shoe?" Nick asked. "Or yours, Caroline?"

I answered for both of us. "No. And some-one took her clock. If it wasn't you, Nick . . ." I paused. "Then someone else has been here."

"There's more to this, isn't there?" Nick asked. "Why don't you sit down and tell us, Marcus."

I told them about the key in the wrong place, the bread, everything. Even the odd feeling I'd had that first morning. "And now the grass prints and the clock," I ended, watching Nick the way I once saw Patchin watch a potato bug. There was nothing to see in Nick's face, no blushing or paling or shifty eyes.

Mom rubbed her forehead. "But why didn't you tell me about the key before, Marcus? I trusted you to act responsibly."

"You were tired all the time. And I wasn't sure."

"You don't have to be sure. We have a deal, the two of us. If you're scared at all . . . if you even suspect something isn't right . . ."

It made it worse that she was getting mad at me in front of Nick. She looked ready to say more but she didn't. Under the table Nick's foot brushed against mine and I realized, knew absolutely, that he'd given Mom a nudge, a warning to go easy and not hassle me anymore. Why did he always have to interfere? Even if I believed him that he hadn't taken any of our stuff—and I wasn't sure I did believe him—he should keep his nose out of our business.

"I suspected something tonight, and you didn't like that much," I said.

"Let's just take another look around," Nick said quietly. "Caroline, would you like to stay here?"

"No. I'm coming with you."

The three of us went again, room to room.

The only thing missing seemed to be the clock.

"I don't *begin* to understand this. Look!" Mom opened the drawer in her bedside table and I saw three small piles of five- and ten-dollar bills with paper clips and notes attached to them. "I got money from the bank yesterday. Last night in bed I was figuring out what the grocery bill would be tomorrow, and putting aside the Christmas money for the paperboy and the mailman. Whoever took the clock didn't look very far. Or wasn't interested."

Something horrible was nagging at my mind, trying to make me listen to it, and suddenly I knew what it was.

"If I had my key with me every second today, how did the person get in? He got in today. The clock was there this morning."

We were in the kitchen again where we'd started.

"The key could have been taken a couple of days ago and a copy made," Nick said. "Then the person could use it to go in and out whenever he wanted."

"But why?" Mom asked. "And why here? Especially when so little was taken. It gives me the creeps."

"Maybe he just happened on that key by luck. Maybe he had nowhere else to go."

Mom shivered. "I can't stand it. Someone *in* here, touching our things, eating our food."

My mind was shifting in dizzying circles. Someone's been sitting in *my* chair. Someone's been sleeping in *my* bed.

"Do you think we should call the police, Marcus?" Mom asked.

I couldn't believe she was asking me and not Nick. Or that he was waiting for me to decide. Of course, that was the way it should be.

"What do you think, Nick?" I definitely couldn't believe *I'd* asked *him.*

"It's not much of a case," Nick said. "One inexpensive clock. The police have too much serious stuff going on. I suspect they'd just tell you to have the locks changed, Caroline."

"I'll have them changed all right. First thing tomorrow morning."

The ringing of the doorbell almost stopped my breathing. "Who on earth?" Mom whispered.

Nick held up his hand. "I'll go."

I went, too, a few paces behind him.

"It's Miss Sarah," he said after he'd looked out the living-room window. She was wearing her plaid robe and a pair of the knitted slippers she and Miss Coriander make and donate to the old people's home.

"We saw the three of you going room to room," she said. "And the house lit up like the Fourth of July. Is something wrong?"

Mom came then and explained about how the clock was missing and what we suspected.

"You mean that cheap, plastic clock you keep by your bed?" I could tell Miss Sarah was wondering if we'd all gone mad.

"Nobody could have come in or out of this house without Coriander or me seeing them. And that's definite!" she said. "We keep an eye on all the comings and goings over here." It seemed to me she was staring accusingly at Nick.

"The back door isn't within your seeing range, Miss Sarah," Nick said. "Not if someone came through the hedge in the other direction."

Miss Sarah gave one of her disbelieving sniffs. "I have to call Coriander," she said. "She's waiting by the phone in case of an emergency. If I don't contact her in three minutes she'll dial 911."

We listened as Miss Sarah gave her sister a full report, sounding as if the whole thing was ridiculous and she expected Miss Coriander to feel the same way.

"We both agree that you and Marcus should not sleep here tonight," she told Mom when she finished. "Get your pajamas and your toothbrush, Marcus. We'll find sheets and pillows and put the two of you in our guest bedroom."

I didn't think Miss Sarah or Miss Coriander could find the *beds* in the guest room, never mind the sheets and pillows. Their whole house is as messy as their kitchen.

"That's not necessary, Miss Sarah," Mom said. "But really, thanks."

"It probably isn't. But if there's the slightest chance that someone does have a key to your house, you're certainly not going to be here if he comes in. Don't be silly, Caroline."

"Why don't I just stay and sleep on the couch tonight?" Nick asked. "That would be the easiest."

Miss Sarah's brown eye and blue eye narrowed and her long nose went up. "It would indeed be *easy*, Mr. Milardovich. But not wise. Caroline would be much safer with us."

I could tell Miss Sarah didn't like the

thought of Mom and Nick being friends any more than I did.

"I think it's a very good idea," Mom said quickly. "Less trouble . . . all around. If you're sure you don't mind the couch, Nick?"

"Looks great to me," Nick said.

"I'm sure!" Somehow Miss Sarah always gets in a parting shot.

So Mom got Nick sheets and a light blanket and a pillow. I have to admit that when I was in bed it was good to think of Nick in the living room. I'd given him the blackthorn stick, and he'd put it on the rug right next to his hand. I lay picturing some faceless person sneaking into our house, moving secretively, quietly, and Nick roaring up from that couch, the blackthorn in his hand, an enraged bear out for blood.

Unless, of course, Nick *was* the faceless person. Then we'd asked the fox to come in and share the chicken coop. But why would he want to? What reason could he possibly have? Anyway, if he had been coming here secretly, he'd been stopped. We'd scared him off. And Miss Sarah and Miss Coriander would be on double guard duty from here on in.

Was he sleeping now?

I tiptoed into the living room.

Nick was snoring softly on the couch. He reminded me of the Santa in the mall with the sign on his stomach. The couch was too short and Nick's hairy legs and knobby feet hung over the end, poking from under the blanket.

It jumped into my head how quick he'd been to say we shouldn't call the police. Quietly I lifted the blackthorn stick from the floor by the couch and took it with me when I went back to bed. No sense leaving him a weapon.

CHAPTER 10

Although she'd borrowed my alarm clock, Mom slept late the next morning. She didn't even have time for a cup of coffee before she left for work. I thought maybe she'd woken up a few times in the night. I had.

It was Nick who had to phone and arrange for the locksmith to come out. While we waited, Nick said he had something for me and he'd run up to his apartment and get it. I thought maybe it was a Christmas gift, but what he had was a set of Campagnolo pedals, packed side by side in a foam-lined box like precious jewels.

"You didn't get them yet, did you?" he asked.

"No. I didn't have time to check with Henry yesterday, though. They might be in."

I couldn't take my eyes off the shine and gleam of the Campies, their classy, elegant lines. "I was going to ride down there this morning."

"I found these in a bike shop over by school," Nick said. "If Henry has yours, I can take them back."

"This was the secret last night?"

"Sure. How could I hand them over in front of your mom?"

I touched the clean, cold metal with the tip of a finger. It was nice of Nick to do this. But he needn't think helping me would make me stop suspecting him. And the pedals were part of the bike, the bike that was my gift to Mom. I'd saved and worked for this all year and I especially didn't want *him* horning in.

"You owe me some bucks," Nick said. "If you want them, that is."

So this was a business arrangement. OK then. "Thanks. I'll be able to get the bike finished this afternoon."

"You're welcome," Nick said.

The locksmith came then. She was young, but seemed to know her stuff, and soon we had new keys for the front and back doors.

"How many will you need?" she asked, looking at Nick.

"Three," I said. "We always leave one for Miss Coriander and Miss Sarah."

Nick held up four fingers. We got four of each. And Nick took the old keys off his ring and slid the new ones on. So maybe the fox still had a key to the chicken coop.

It was already ten o'clock and I called Henry, half hoping the Campies would be there, waiting for me in his shop, so I could ask Nick to take his back. Getting them from Nick did make a difference, no matter how I tried to make myself believe it didn't. But they hadn't come, and Henry told me he didn't expect a delivery tomorrow, Christmas Eve. "I'm real sorry, Marcus," he said. "Why don't you come down and I'll find you the next best thing?"

"I don't need the next best thing," I said. "I've got the best."

Henry said, "Buying from the competition, huh?" Then he said, "Great, Marcus. And don't worry about the ones you ordered. I can sell them and get bigger bucks too. I always lose out on cash when I sell to a friend."

It's true. Henry always does give me a good deal.

For the rest of the day I worked in the garage, putting the pedals on the bike, polishing everything with special wax. The Campies looked great! Talk about the finishing touch! Talk about the "piece de" whatever! Those Campies did it. The bike looked like a million dollars.

I called Robbie to come over and see.

"I bet you could sell this baby for fifty bucks," he said when he came.

"Shoot," I told him. "The pedals alone cost close to that."

"A hundred." He began humming and looking at me sideways.

"This bike's for my mom, you bozo."

"I know that. I just mean, if she gets *tired* of it. Or doesn't use it or something."

"She'll use it," I said. "This is a custom job. A real Rolls Royce of a bike."

Robbie was sitting on the floor over Sydney with his feet covering Perth. I'd told him all about last night and the missing clock. He'd examined the grass clump, sniffing it, holding it up to his ear.

"It's not *ticking*, Robbie," I said.

"Maybe we should take it to one of those police labs," he'd suggested.

I'd told him about Nick sleeping over and the extra key. I tell Robbie just about everything. But I didn't mention seeing Anjelica Trotter in the mall. Robbie would have loved hearing about how different she'd looked, and he'd have had all kinds of funny reasons for her flat top. I could even imagine. But I didn't want to tell him.

He'd brought over my Christmas present, which was soft to the squeeze, like toilet paper on TV. "It isn't something to wear, is it?" I asked.

Robbie nodded. "You'll like it, though. It's not ordinary, I'll tell you that."

After he left I thought it only fair to invite Nick down to see the bike too.

He walked all around it, his head cocked on one side. "Great job, Marcus," he said, and I knew he meant it. You can tell about things like that.

"I still have to get the money out of my savings account for you," I told him. "I don't think I can do that now till after Christmas."

"No hurry," he said.

But there was a hurry. For me anyway. I wanted to get him paid. "As soon as I can," I promised.

It was five o'clock and already growing dark. I went inside and took a shower. Ages ago I'd seen a movie called *Psycho*, about a lady who got stabbed in a shower. I began thinking about that while the water was running on me and I almost busted a gut to get out and dry off. But the new locks were on the doors. I was safe. Safe and secure in my own house the way I'd always been. Wasn't I?

I was in the kitchen fixing a salad and thinking about Anjelica Trotter when I heard the smallest of sounds in the garage. I stopped, my hands still in the bowl, with bits of lettuce and spinach stuck between my fingers and salad oil all the way up to my wrists. What was that? A hiss, a small bump, a jingling. It was as if someone was in there, had stubbed a toe against the workbench. It wasn't enough of a sound to hear normally, but I realized, even though the locks were changed and the only thing missing for sure was a dumb old clock, that I'd been semilistening all day. Semiwatching too. I'd been peeking over my shoulder as I worked on the bike, going often to the living-room window to look down the driveway.

I took my hands from the salad bowl, wiped them on my jeans, tiptoed to the door, and put my ear against the paneled wood. At first I could hear only my heart, or maybe the blood running scared through my body. But then I knew there was someone in the garage, moving quietly, tiptoeing the way I'd tiptoed across the kitchen. I'd been here all the time. How did he get in? Through the garage door. That was the sound I'd heard, the heavy weight going up, the swish, the faint creak of the hinges. Someone was in there!

Quick as anything I flung open the kitchen door, snaked my hand round the side into the garage, and pushed on the light switch. At the same time I pressed myself flat against the kitchen wall. Little by little I wormed my head around.

When the garage door goes up on the automatic opener, a light comes on attached to the center hinge. I'd forgotten that. It stays on for about two minutes before it goes off. I think it's supposed to let you see to get out of your car, or be safe when you open the door and the garage is dark.

Now both lights were on. And there was someone there all right. He was standing in the middle of the garage staring at me. If ever anyone, anytime, looked guilty, he did.

"Nick!" I said. "What are you doing? How did you get the big door up?"

He answered the second question, but not the first. "I have one of your automatic openers," he said. He did. It was right there in his hand. His other was hidden behind his back. "Your mother has two, you know. She lent me one so—"

"So you could use the washer and dryer," I said nastily. "That must have been before she gave you the key. My mom sure is nice to you."

"Yes, she is. She's very nice."

"You scared the heck out of me," I said. "What have you got behind your back?"

"Where?"

"Behind your back. Don't tell me it's your dirty laundry." Big bear creature, standing there with his thick legs spread apart. With a click the automatic light went off. Two minutes.

I began walking toward him. "Let me see."

"Sorry, Marcus. I can't do that."

I stopped a few paces in front of him. "I'm going to tell Mom about you," I said. The words were so whiny and babyish that I wished them back as soon as I'd spoken them.

"Look," Nick said, "I'm sorry I scared you. I just didn't think you'd hear. Man, you have some great ears on you!" He smiled but I didn't smile back.

"I thought you didn't come in here secretly," I said.

"Let's say this time's an exception. And I don't think it would be a good idea to tell your mother about it."

"Oh, you don't." There was a thick, hard lump in my throat. "Well you just quit sneaking around our place. From now on, stay out of our garage. And out of our house." I wanted to add, "And out of our lives," but that sounded too nerdy.

I ran back up the steps, slammed off the light, and locked the kitchen door behind me.

It was a few minutes before I heard the faint

creak and swish as the big door closed. What had he been doing? I should have stayed instead of jamming out like that. Was he inside now or out?

Out.

From around the side of the living-room drapes I watched him lope up the steps to his apartment. Whatever he carried in front of him was hidden by the breadth of his back. He had taken something. He *was* the one. I could tell Mom now and she would believe me.

So why was I feeling so rotten?

CHAPTER 11

When I woke up Christmas Eve morning I didn't feel happy the way I do most Christmas Eves. It took a while to remember why: Nick, and last night.

Mom was in the kitchen eating a toasted muffin and jelly and drinking coffee.

"Want some?" she asked.

"No thanks." I got out the fruit-and-bran cereal and a dish.

Mom watched me over the top of her coffee mug. "It's such a pain having to work Christmas Eve," she said. "But I'll be home at five and then Christmas will really begin."

"I know." On the table there was a bowl of red roses that Miss Coriander had sent over. Mom loves roses and Miss Coriander is about the only one who has them this time of year.

"Nick won't be home today," she said.

"Too bad," I muttered, pouring cereal into my dish.

"But if you feel the least bit . . ." She paused and then started over. "If you feel too much alone, go next door. Everything's safe, of course, with the new locks. But Miss Sarah and Miss Coriander will be starting their cooking today. You might want to see what they're doing." Miss Sarah and Miss Coriander always bring a ton of food when they come for Christmas dinner, including creamed onions and spinach soufflé and their special molded salads filled with nuts and cranberries. They won't take the leftovers home, either, so Mom and I eat our way right into New Year's.

"You could learn to make that spinach soufflé," she said. "Then we wouldn't have to wait until Christmas every year to have it."

"I thought maybe I'd ask Robbie to come over, if that's OK."

"Sure. Good idea. But you two monkeys stay away from under the tree. No untying the gifts and checking them out then tying them up again."

"Mom! We were nine years old."

"No switching labels!" she added.

"We were ten!"

"So now you're thirteen. Stay away."

"Party pooper," I said.

A small pitcher of milk was on the table and I poured some on my cereal, careful not to look at her. "Mom? Last night Nick was in the garage."

"Marcus! Are you going to start—"

"You said to tell you if something was bothering me. You said I had a responsibility."

Her voice softened. "I know. You're right."

"I didn't want to bring it up again. I didn't mention it last night because I wanted to think it through. But . . . but . . . and now he has a key again."

Mom stood up. She looked pale and she said something quietly that I couldn't quite hear, something like "This isn't going to work, Caroline." To me she said: "I'll ask him to give the key back, Marcus. See you tonight."

I took a quick look around the garage after she left. Nothing seemed to be missing. Then

Robbie came, and he and I shot baskets for a while. Afterward we lay on our backs on my bed, a package of Fig Newtons between us, a pitcher of lemonade on the floor.

"You're sure he took something?" Robbie asked.

"Pretty sure."

He sat up so suddenly, the bed bounced and my plastic glass of lemonade sloshed over my bare stomach between my T-shirt and jeans. "Not your mom's bike?" he asked.

"No, goofball!" I grabbed a Kleenex to sop up the mess. "It couldn't have been anything that big."

Robbie plunked back down. "But what's in the garage? I mean that anybody would want?"

"Tools. My spare bike parts. Boxes of stuff for the Goodwill. The ladder. The lawn mower."

"Well, he sure didn't hide those behind his back." Robbie paused. "You think your mom's going to marry him?"

"Sometimes you get the craziest ideas, Robbie."

Robbie giggled. "If she did, your name

would be Marcus Milardovich. You'd sound like a Russian spy."

"You think it sounds weirder than Robert Roberts?"

"*I* think it does."

I gave him a look. "It's not going to happen. Anyway, I'd *never* change my name."

"OK, OK." Robbie lifted one foot and flicked a piece of dirt from the sole of his Nikes. I picked the dirt crumbles from my bedcover and made a face.

"Did I tell you my cousin Jimmy plays on Nick's team?" Robbie asked.

"About a hundred times you told me."

"Did I tell you how they had this real mean assistant coach and he told the guys to crawl on their hands and knees after they lost a game and how Nick exploded and yelled—"

"And told the guys to get up, they weren't animals, and then he fired the coach—"

"The assistant coach," Robbie corrected. "His name was Mr. Clipper."

"You've told me all that a hundred times, too," I said.

"That was pretty nice of Nick, huh? Jimmy says all the guys like him a lot. Jimmy likes him."

"Listen," I said. "Nick's probably different at work and at home. That doesn't mean anything. Anyway, I happen to know he's not going to be around today. Usually he leaves his door unlocked, so I might just go up there and see what I can find." I made myself sound real casual. "Mostly I'm looking for a clock. Or whatever he took from our garage. Mostly I'm looking for proof."

Robbie's eyes sparkled. "Great idea, Marcus. A search-and-destroy mission."

"I don't know about the destroy. Wait a sec." I went to the window to check and I saw that Nick's car was still there. "I'll have to wait," I told Robbie, sliding down on the floor with my back against the bed. Robbie was chugging lemonade straight from the pitcher, with a sound like water flushing down a drain. He wiped his mouth on the end of my bedcover. "Guess who I saw this morning?"

"Don't do that," I said. "I have to sleep under that bedcover. Who did you see?"

"Anjelica Trotter."

I kept a poker expression, although it was hard.

"She was riding her bike along your street."

"Yeah?" I examined the wet patch on the bedcover.

"Where do you think she was going?" Robbie asked.

"I have no idea." Even the top of my head was burning, but I managed to sound real cool. "How did she look?"

Robbie did a round curving thing with his hands on the front of his T-shirt. "Another two inches, I swear! Anjelica Trotter's top is a total miracle."

"Total," I agreed. If only he knew!

"I bet she—" Robbie began.

Outside my window was the sound of Nick starting up his Dodge. "We're in business, Robbie," I interrupted happily. "Here's where the action starts."

But pretty soon I realized it wasn't going to be easy to get up Nick's stairs without Miss Sarah or Miss Coriander spotting me. I'd forgotten about them. There was no way to get the action started. Every time I'd wander out toward the back, there they'd be mixing things or peeling things at their counter by the window. They'd wave and I'd wave back and retreat.

"It's like trying to get past a sentry box," I told Robbie.

But after lunch Miss Sarah came out and opened the trunk of their Buick, and she and her sister began carrying out green branches and pots of poinsettias and chrysanthemums.

"The plants are for Christmas Eve midnight mass, Robbie," I said. "They'll be loading for a while. And then Miss Sarah will drive the stuff over and come back. I'll go now, while they're busy. Keep watch."

"I'll signal if I see Nick coming home," Robbie said. "I'll whistle."

Of course I wouldn't need a signal. The first thing we'd see would be Nick's Dodge cruising up the driveway, and then it would be too late. "Just throw yourself in front of his car," I said. "That'll work better."

"You don't think anyone will come in here while you're gone, do you?" Robbie asked, jerking his head this way and that, like a nervous chicken.

"No. I told you. All the locks were changed. If someone does, *then* you can whistle."

I raced up Nick's steps. What if this time he *had* locked the door? He should. But if he was

Mr. Fox in person, he'd know he didn't have to.

The door was open. I slid inside and closed it behind me.

The apartment was flooded with sunlight.

I checked the stuff on the table beside the couch first. No clock. Well, would I expect him to have it where Mom or I might see it? I'd need to open drawers and closets to check properly, and that would be hard to do. I felt like a crumbum even thinking about it.

"But if he's a thief . . ." I said out loud. "Besides, he said I should come up anytime." Not to look through his private things, though. He hadn't invited me to do that. So?

I opened the drawer on the bedside table and pawed through his stuff. I checked the closet. The top shelf was filled with packages, Christmas wrapped. Maybe he'd hidden something behind them.

I dragged over the wicker chair and lifted the packages out. There were tags on all of them and they were all for Blake, whoever that was. Most of the wrapping paper was faded and torn as though the packages had been around for a long time. There was a new one, though, big and square, wrapped in green foil with a green ribbon. The white, stuck-on card said *To Blake* again. Weird! Then I found a small, square box in the same kind of green foil marked "To Caroline with love from Nick." With love to my mother! I jammed it all the way back where there was nothing but dust. There hadn't been anything in that pile for me. Well, Nick wasn't on my Christmas list either.

The closet-sized bathroom smelled of Nick. The mat by the shower still had two great, damp bear prints on it. I almost hung up the towel he'd left in a wet heap on the floor, but I remembered in time not to move it. That would have been a mistake. Anyway, I wasn't here to pick up after him.

Back to the living room. A wicker chest with a broken brass hasp on top was filled with records and books and photographs. Some of the pictures were framed. Most of them were of a kid with blond curly hair and big blue eyes. In one he was about two, in another one a bit older. I turned the picture over. Printed on the back were the words "Blake, age two years two months." So that was the Blake on all those old Christmas presents. But why were they still in Nick's closet? I flipped over all the pictures. There was one at age five where he looked exactly like Nick. Poor kid, I thought. In a couple of them he was with a woman whose name on the back was Anne. Anne and Blake at age three. And then I found one with a trio: Nick, Anne, and Blake. Blake was six, according to the label on the back. The date placed it as being taken seven years ago. So Blake would be thirteen now, same as me.

Nick didn't have his beard back then. He looked kind of young himself, and he was smiling down at Blake in such a soft, loving way it made my throat hurt. I remembered Dad looking at me like that. Some people say I'm lucky that I was eight when my dad died so I can remember him, but I'm not sure about that. If you didn't remember, it wouldn't hurt so much not to have him anymore. I stared at the picture for a long time before I put it away with the others, trying to remember what order they were in. I don't think there was any order. Nothing else. No place left to look. I didn't want to anyway.

When I opened Nick's door a crack I could see Miss Coriander stooped over her kitchen counter. Oh no! She's not quite the spotter that Miss Sarah is, but close. She'd see me for sure coming down the steps. And she'd want to know why, and she'd just mention it to Mom the way they'd mentioned once seeing me ride my bike through a red light. And Mom would say, "Are you spying on Nick? Is that what you're doing?"

Robbie was leaning against the side of our house out of Miss Coriander's range, waving his arms to get my attention. When I waved back he pointed warningly at her window, then at himself, then toward the front of the house, before he disappeared. I waited.

One of my shoelaces was untied and I tied it again. Miss Sarah used to tell me all the time to tie my laces. "You'll trip and chip your front teeth, Marcus. Miss Coriander and I knew a boy. . . ." I might have to run and I didn't want to trip.

In a few minutes I heard the Clarks' front doorbell. It has a very loud ring so neither Miss Sarah nor Miss Coriander will miss it. That bell's so loud even deaf old Patchin across the street hears it, and it gets him very excited. Miss Sarah and Miss Coriander also have squawk boxes all over their house so they can ask who's there, and the person who rings talks into a little round microphone thing and states his business.

Robbie's voice came like an echo through a tunnel.

"It's Robert Roberts, Miss Coriander. I'm Marcus' friend."

As soon as Miss Coriander headed for the front door I ran down the steps and back in our house.

"That was pretty smart," I told Robbie when he came back. Not that I needed to tell him. He was saying, "How about that? Huh? What did you think of *that* for a trick?" He'd have been patting himself on the back if he could have reached.

"What did you say when she came to the door?" I asked.

"I took her those roses that were on your table and told her I hoped she'd have a real nice Christmas," Robbie said.

"She *gave* us those roses. She grows them."

"So? She didn't recognize them. Now she

doesn't have to pick any for herself. What did you find in Nick's?"

"Nothing of ours. The place is clean. Maybe Nick is really OK."

I was thinking of Anne and Nick and Blake, that softness in Nick's face, and I was feeling lousy again. Did Mom know about them? And where was the photograph I'd seen of her the first time? It wasn't around now.

"Are you sure there was nothing?" Robbie asked.

"I'm sure."

"Why don't we check your garage again," he suggested. "I've got a great eye. Maybe I'll see something missing that you missed."

"That's got to be the all-time wackiest sentence," I said.

We did a real thorough job in the garage. Or at least I thought we did. But I'd forgotten one thing that I'd put out there because it took up too much room in my closet. And it wasn't till later that I remembered it and realized it had disappeared too.

CHAPTER 12

Robbie went home in the afternoon, taking the gift I'd bought for him. It was a Nerf Frisbee. Nerf Frisbees are great. I've been wanting one for a long time, and giving one to your friend is like getting one for yourself.

"I hope your mom likes her present and that you get a lot of super stuff," Robbie said when he left.

"Yeah, thanks. Say Merry Christmas to everybody from me."

When he'd gone, I took out a soft cloth and polished Mom's bike and rubbed the Campies till they sparkled like sunlight. I tied a great bow on the handlebars before I went back inside. There was a game show on TV with a wheel and a ball and people jumping around. I watched for a while, trying not to think of

Nick and Blake. At four thirty I got up to switch the set off and peer out the window, something I seem to be doing on a regular basis these days. Anjelica Trotter was on my front porch. First came the fright and then the excitement, and before I knew what I was doing, I knocked on the window glass.

Anjelica jumped as if a firecracker had gone off at her feet. She stared at me and I stared at her. It was weird, because although she was back to looking like the scary grown-up Anjelica Trotter again, I wasn't scared at all. I could still picture the mall Anjelica hidden underneath.

"Anjelica, wait," I mouthed, and dashed for the front door.

When I opened it we were staring at one another again. "Oh, ah, hi, Marcus," she said. She was wearing red shorts, a striped red-and-white shirt, and her red-and-green "Color Me Christmas" lipstick. Lots of it. The shirt was very bulgy in front, and I quickly decided Robbie was right about the extra two inches.

"Hi." I tugged at the sides of my T-shirt, tucking them more neatly into my jeans. "Ah, so what's happening, Anjelica?"

"Nothing. I was just, you know, riding by." Her neck was getting a funny spotted pink. Maybe her face was, too, underneath all the junk she had on it. There was a white envelope in her hand. I glanced down at it and saw my name printed on the front. "I was just delivering this," she said, and shoved it at me. She'd put a Santa sticker where the stamp should have been.

"Good idea," I said. "You can't be sure about the mails this time of year. It's great to save postage." I was secretly feeling around the envelope. This wasn't just a card. There was something else in here, something small and bulky. A Christmas present, probably. And I had nothing for her. How embarrassing! I opened the door a little wider. "Would you like to come in?"

"I thought you weren't allowed to have visitors," she said in her old simpery way. I almost got scared again.

"I think it's all right. Because it's Christmas. And because my mom knows you now."

"Well, OK. Should I just leave my bike here?"

"That's fine."

She passed me in a wave of perfume.

We stood in the hallway and I was thinking: What next? Anjelica Trotter in my house! What would Robbie say?

"You look very nice," I muttered, insincerely.

"Thank you. I could have just died in the mall. I mean, I looked so awful, and then to meet you! The thing is, my parents don't allow me to wear makeup. Not eye liner or lipstick or anything. They're so old-fashioned. So I have to make myself look good when they're not around. Thank goodness they both leave the house before I do in the mornings, or you could guess how nerdy I'd look in school!"

"Oh," I said. "*I* thought you looked really nice at the mall. I mean really, *really* nice." I was making a mess out of this. "Nicer than normal, even," I added.

"Oh sure." Anjelica bent her head, examining our hall rug or else the red-and-green laces in her tennies.

"No, I did think that." I nodded and nodded to show how sincere I was. "I like girls with ordinary faces."

"Ordinary?"

"I mean plain. No, not plain . . . I didn't mean plain. Just without gunk on them."

"Gunk?"

"Is it hot in here?" I asked. "I think maybe I turned on the heat by mistake. Do you want some juice?"

"I guess."

I led the way to the kitchen, put the envelope on the table, and got two glasses from the cupboard. "We have orange or cranberry."

"Orange please." Anjelica hovered behind me.

I carried the glasses to the table and said politely, "Would you like to sit?"

She sat across from me, her hands curled around the glass. She had nice short, bitten nails, like mine, and fat little hands. Wow, I thought. Me and Anjelica having a drink together. Wait till I tell Robbie.

She stared around the kitchen. "Your house is pretty."

"It's OK."

"Do you want to open your present now?" she asked, looking down at the envelope.

Criminy! So it was a present. "If you want. Mom and I usually open all our gifts tonight. I was going to keep yours."

"I kind of want to see if you like it."

"Well, sure." I turned the envelope over. Across the flap were printed the letters *IWAKFC* and underneath the words: "You can ask me what this means."

"So what does it mean?" I asked.

She was starting to blush again. "Oh nothing. Just ignore that. I was planning on leaving it, you see. I didn't expect you to read it, not in front of me."

"Oh, OK." I ran my fingers under the glue, being careful not to tear the letters, which I planned on figuring out later. Inside was a small, sealed plastic envelope filled with stamps. "I've been collecting these for you for ages," Anjelica said. "I remembered your display at open house."

When I shook the envelope the stamps slithered around and I could see lots that I already had. I probably had all of them actually, since my collection is pretty extensive.

"My gran gave me this one." Anjelica pointed through the plastic to a pink Italian

Rocca Maggiore Assisi stamp, which is really common. "A friend of hers is in Rome. She sent Gran a card."

I'd had three of those that I'd traded at the last flea market. But of course I didn't tell Anjelica that. "It's great. They're all great," I said.

Our glasses were empty. Anjelica's had red-and-green smears around the rim. I guess she leaves her "Color Me Christmas" trademark wherever she goes.

"Well," I said.

"Well." Anjelica stood up.

I stood too, still holding the envelope. "I'm sorry I didn't get you anything for Christmas, Anjelica. I didn't know I'd be seeing you."

She gave me the strangest look, sort of shy and sort of soppy. "I ride up and down your street a lot when I've got nothing better to do."

Now it was my turn to blush. I could feel the burning even in my ears. She was telling me she *liked* me, telling me out loud, with just the two of us here!

"Well, Merry Christmas, Marky."

Criminy! I hoped she didn't start calling me

Marky in school. Robbie would die laughing.

"You too. Merry Christmas. And thanks again for the stamps."

I watched her walk across the porch and down the steps. In a minute she'd be gone. She was almost at her bike. I *could* tell her about that guy Garcia from the chorus who wanted her to call, but I didn't. Let him find her himself. I stared desperately down at the envelope. *IWAKFC.* Think fast, Marcus, think.

"Anjelica?" I called. "I've got it."

"Got what?"

I jumped the steps from the top to the ground, showing off a bit. "The letters. Do they mean: 'In Western Australia Kingfishers Favor Cod'?"

Anjelica laughed. She looked nice when she laughed, especially now that a whole lot of her Christmas lipstick was on the glass and not on her. "That's not what it means," she said.

"I didn't really think so. It's just, Robbie and I have a map of Australia in the garage, so I'm sort of Australia minded. Would you like to see it? The map? We've got Oodnadatta in there. It's a famous town, right in the middle."

"Sure." Anjelica stepped away from her bike.

"Wait a sec," I said. I had to rush back inside to push the button to open the garage door. She was still there when I came out.

I showed her Australia and how you could step from Sydney to Perth. "A distance of over 2000 miles," I said, "as the crow flies. Or the kookaburra. That's an Australian bird that laughs. I have one on a stamp."

Anjelica looked impressed.

I showed her Mom's bike in detail and she was impressed even more.

She fingered the big red bow and stroked the shine of the racing handlebars. "I'd really like these kind on my bike," she said. Before I realized what I was doing I was telling her how I'd found these in Henry's trash and how I'd start looking for her if she wanted. How I'd even put them on for her, sort of a late Christmas present.

"Could you? That would be great," Anjelica said.

"Nick got the special pedals for me." I hadn't meant to say that either.

"Who's Nick?"

I spun both pedals at once. "Oh, nobody. A friend of my mother's." I pictured him again in the photograph, smiling down at his son, and I didn't know how I felt. Sad? Angry? I couldn't possibly be jealous, could I? "He's really just a paying tenant," I said.

Anjelica and I stood facing each other, shuffling around like a couple of kookaburras getting ready to dance. "I like your garage," Anjelica said.

"It's very comfortable." I flicked my nail against the envelope. "Do you want to tell me what the letters mean now?"

Anjelica studied her tennies again and I joined her. We both watched her toes wiggle under the red canvas. "I'll call you sometime and tell you," she said at last.

"OK."

I walked her to her bike and inspected the handlebars in a very professional way. "These will be real easy to take off, soon as I get the new ones. So. See you after Christmas."

When she was well out of hearing distance, I leaped up to touch an overhanging jacaranda branch and yelled, "All right! Way to go, Marcus!"

"Marcus!" The voice was so close and so loud it made me jump again, although not as high. It was only Miss Sarah on the other side of the hedge. All I could see were her eyes and the tip of her nose. "What on earth are you whooping and hollering about, Marcus?"

"Oh, nothing."

The blue eye and the brown eye examined me carefully. "Is that girl a friend of yours from school?"

"Yes. She's in a couple of my classes."

"Oh." Miss Sarah can put more into one word than anybody I know. I wanted to laugh, imagining the way it had probably been. Chances are Miss Coriander had spotted Anjelica as soon as she came up on my porch.

"Sarah!" she'd have gasped the way she does. "Sarah, a *girl* just went into Marcus' house."

"A *girl*?"

"A very mature-looking girl. What should we do, Sarah? She and Marcus are *all alone.*"

"I'll just go out there, Coriander. I'll be on the other side of the hedge, and if the girl screams for help . . ."

"Of if Marcus screams for help, Sarah . . ."

"Is everything all right, Marcus?" Miss Sarah asked, watching me closely.

"Everything's fine."

"Be sure to lock up carefully behind you when you go in, Marcus. And don't forget to close the garage door."

"I won't. Thanks."

"See you tomorrow."

I went inside, turned the lock real hard so she'd be sure to hear it click, swung the garage door down. In the kitchen I kept the envelope propped in front of me as I washed and dried the glasses. *IWAKFC.* If wishes and kookaburras . . . The *K* could stand for *kiss.* I almost dropped the glass.

Soon it would be dark. I wandered into the living room, lit the lamps, and turned on the tree lights. Mom would be home in a while and Christmas Eve with all its traditions would start. First we'd trim the tree and open the gifts. And tonight I'd sleep next to the tree the way I always do Christmas Eve, warm in my sleeping bag, smelling the cold forest smells, imagining . . . I stopped imagining before I began. Where *was* my sleeping bag? I'd taken it out of my closet and stashed it in the garage a couple of weeks ago. I'd forgotten that when Robbie and I'd checked the garage earlier. Was it still there? I couldn't remember. I couldn't remember when I'd last seen it.

I went back in the kitchen, opened the garage, and turned on the light. On the workbench was the big bag of potting soil, the pile of clay pots, and the oil can. The tools hung neatly from the pegboard above. No sleeping bag. It was too big to miss, but I went out and moved everything anyway, checking. The sleeping bag was gone.

CHAPTER 13

I knew for sure Nick hadn't taken the sleeping bag from the garage yesterday. Whatever he'd had behind his back had been small and easily hidden. And if the bag had been in his apartment I'd have found it. Besides, why would he want it? Why would he want any of this stuff? I had to face what I didn't want to face and what I'd begun to suspect for the last couple of days. There'd been a thief who had used my key, come into our house, and helped himself to whatever he wanted. The thief was not Nick. I'd wanted it to be Nick, for reasons of my own. It just hadn't worked out.

I went back into the house. Better not to mention the missing sleeping bag to Mom. Not tonight. Not on Christmas Eve. I'd make some excuse for not sleeping under the tree, and I'd try to be nicer to Nick, at least until

Christmas was over. I'd try for Mom's sake, and because I'd been unfair.

It's hard, though, to change yourself drastically.

I heard Nick's car drive up, and a couple of seconds later he rang our doorbell. He was carrying two packages, one small and one large and flat. The small one I'd seen before in his apartment. It was Mom's.

"Lose your key?" I asked halfheartedly. It wasn't as easy to hate him now that I'd seen the pictures of him with Anne and Blake.

"No. I didn't lose it. Your Mom thought it might be better if I didn't have a key to the house," he said. "No problem."

"Oh." I'd won a victory, but I didn't feel very happy about it.

He held out the packages. "Christmas gifts for you and your mom."

"Oh," I said again, stuck on the silly word. I looked at the packages without taking them. "Don't you want to bring them when you come for Christmas dinner?"

"Your mom says you open your gifts tonight. I wanted these to be part of your opening."

"She's not home yet. Do you want to come

in?" My tone of voice let him know I definitely didn't want him to.

"No, Marcus. The two of you should have your Christmas Eve to yourselves. But thanks for asking me."

Now I felt really bad. "OK," I said. "Well, thanks for the gifts." I stood, not closing the door. "You know what, Nick? When that guy came and took the clock, he took my sleeping bag from the garage too."

"He did?" Nick shook his head. "He took some weird things, that's for sure. You know what, Marcus? I think we should stop thinking about that creep and not let him spoil Christmas."

I nodded. "I've stopped."

When Mom came, I told her about Nick and the gifts and she smiled and looked pleased. "I got him a Walkman radio from both of us," she said. "So he can listen to his Mozart tapes while he jogs."

"His Mozart tapes?" Was there anything about Nick that Mom didn't know? I waited for my slow burn of resentment to start, but tonight I had to help it along a bit. "Do you know about Nick's wife and kid?" I asked, watching her carefully.

"A bit. He doesn't say much. He and his wife were divorced when Blake was six. His wife got custody. She was supposed to allow Nick to visit his son but she took off, illegally. Nick's been searching for the last seven years and has never found a trace of them."

I remembered the pile of wrapped and undelivered Christmas presents Nick had in his closet.

"She must have hated Nick a lot to have run off like that."

"Some divorces are really bitter, Marcus. And often without much reason. It's sad."

"Nick was probably rotten," I said, but that halfhearted unsureness was back in my voice.

"I don't believe Nick would know how to be rotten," Mom said. Then she smiled. "So? How about you and I getting Christmas Eve started?"

I shrugged. "Fine with me."

First we went out again, driving the four blocks to Jimmy Joe's market to pick up our fresh turkey and oysters. He keeps the turkey for us till the last minute because we don't have room for such a big beast in our refrigerator.

"Twenty-two pounds," he said. "And a fine figure of a bird."

We wished each other Merry Christmas and drove home.

After Mom put the food away, she went to her room to change. I stood by the tree, staring around. I had the creepy crawlies again. There was a feeling in the room, an alien presence. I thought I saw a shadow move against the wall. "Is anybody there?" I whispered, peering into the corner.

Of course nobody was there. It was only the tree shape, dark and changing in the twinkling lights.

"Just quit it, Marcus," I said out loud. "You're making your head crazy. There's nobody there. The thief has been and gone. Forget him."

"Have you started talking to yourself now, hon?" Mom asked, coming back in the room.

"Oh, just once in a while," I said.

She'd changed into her raspberry-colored cords and her big, loose raspberry sweatshirt. Her black hair was tied back with a pink-and-silver ribbon.

"You look very nice," I told her, which was

what I'd said to Anjelica Trotter. But this time I meant it.

Mom fixed her creamy oyster stew, which probably tastes so wonderful because we have it only on Christmas Eve. We sat across from one another at the table and the thought of Nick upstairs, alone in his little room, drifted into my mind. I made it drift out again.

Mom pointed with her fork to the blue vase. "What happened to Miss Coriander's roses?"

I'd pulled a few pieces of ivy from the backyard to fill the vase, but Mom is not dumb and ivy does not look or smell like roses.

"Robbie took them," I said. "He wanted to give them to somebody."

Mom's eyes opened wide. "A girl?"

"Sort of," I said.

"Oh well. I guess they went in a good cause."

I lingered over my stew, making it last, not wanting to move on to the next part of our Christmas Eve ritual, the one where I go up to the attic and bring down the box of decorations for the tree.

Usually I don't mind the attic. It's half floored and we use it for storage. Where the planking ends you can look beyond, down into the empty, cobwebby dark where dust drifts between the studs and up into the shadowy peak of the roof.

I've never been allowed to play up there.

"Your dad had plans for this," Mom told me once. "We were going to have a rec room, all paneled, with a Ping-Pong table and an old jukebox. Your dad always wanted one of those jukeboxes so we could play old Donovan records and dance the way we used to. Donovan was our favorite. But of course we never got the rec room or the jukebox."

I wished they had. I wouldn't have minded going up into that kind of place. I don't usually mind this one either. But the way things had been going, I wasn't anxious to poke my head into anywhere dark and out of the way.

"Is it time to trim the tree?" Mom asked after we'd done the dishes.

"I guess," I said. "I'll get the flashlight."

It wasn't in the kitchen drawer where we keep it.

"It has to be there," Mom said. "I saw it yesterday. You're not looking properly."

I was. And it wasn't there. I checked the

next drawer, pawing through pot holders and drying cloths, and then I stood very still, staring out at the darkness beyond the kitchen window. The crazy thief had taken the flashlight, too.

"We'll find it sometime when we don't need it," Mom said, and I wondered if she knew we'd never find it and why—if we were trying to protect one another from remembering that there'd been a stranger here, prowling around inside our house.

"Can you make do with my penlight?" she asked.

When I nodded she got it from her purse. "I think I'll just come with you." Her eyes didn't quite meet mine.

"You'll be sneezing all night if you do," I said. "That's prehistoric dust up there. Besides, all I have to do is reach in. The box is right at the top."

As I climbed, though, she stood halfway up the attic steps, partly so I could pass the big, awkward carton down to her, and partly to make going into the attic easier for me. As I said, my mom is not dumb.

I opened the hatch and shone the thin beam into the darkness. The moving light picked up the trunk that had been Dad's in college, the cedar closet where Mom keeps her heavy going-to-visit-Grandma coat, the single-bed mattress, and my old rocking horse, too dear for Mom to part with. The narrow shaft was no more than a small searchlight in the sky, so skinny, so nothing, making the dark around it deeper and more mysterious.

"I thought the box was right here," I called down to Mom. "It's not. We must have moved it."

I climbed up and onto the floor. There was a strange smell. What was it? Something I'd smelled before, something holy, or of Christmas. Just the smell of the cedar closet? No time to stand here, sniffing the dank air, not with the dark pressing against me and the small shuffles and creaks. There was the box of Christmas ornaments. I slipped the flashlight into the pocket of my T-shirt and was immediately in blackness except for the square of light coming through the hatch.

Around me the attic seemed to breathe . . . in, out, in, out.

Mom's voice floated up. "Did you find it, Marcus?"

"Yes." I lifted the box, stumbling in my

hurry to get out. Mom grabbed it as I eased it down the steps and immediately started to sneeze.

"See?" I asked. "It's a good thing you didn't come up."

We carried the box into the living room, where the tree waited, where the dark was safely closed away.

Mom has tapes of Christmas music, and we put them on and took out the old ornaments, one by one. There were the pearl drops with half the pearling worn off . . . the snowflakes I'd made in third grade. Everything came with its own remembering. "Remember when Grandma bought you this little horse? And here's the choo-choo train."

I wouldn't let myself even glance at the corner where I thought I'd seen the shadow move. Is anybody there? Nobody. Nobody's there.

The music moved around us, the choir voices building and soaring to their final hallelujahs.

The angel was in her own small drawstring bag, cushioned in yellowed tissue paper. I took her out.

"Your dad used to have to lift you up to put

her on top of the tree," Mom said.

I still needed the stool.

When I clipped her on, her wing shadow spread across the ceiling like a blessing in church.

In an hour it would be Christmas.

"Shall we open those gifts?" Mom asked, squeezing my hand.

"Yes," I said. "But can I give you yours first?"

"I think I'll die if you don't," she said. "You'll never know how many times I was tempted to peer over and see what was behind that sheet."

I took her arm. "Come with me and close your eyes." I opened the door between the kitchen and garage and put on the light.

"Stay here and keep those eyes closed," I warned as I whipped the cover off and wheeled her gorgeous, handmade custom bike close.

"Now!" I watched her face, the way her eyes widened and the joy in her smile.

"Oh Marcus," she said. "Are you going to tell me you made this beautiful thing entirely yourself?"

I stuck out my chest. "It was nothing."

Mom got on the bike and rode it round and round the garage, across the length and breadth of Australia. Then she stopped under the light to admire it bit by bit.

"I can hardly wait till tomorrow to try it," she said. "Let's ride before breakfast, OK?"

"OK."

Before we went back in she bent and kissed the handlebars and said, "'Bye, bike."

Sometimes Mom does a baby thing like that, and it always makes me laugh.

"Now we'll get your present from me," she said. "Not that it can compare."

She'd bought me what I'd suspected and hoped for . . . a complete tool set with everything in it that I could possibly need for a lifetime of bike making. Ratchets, sockets, screwdrivers, wrenches, pliers, hex-key set! The green metal carrying case had my initials in black. M.M. Marcus Mullen. Or Marcus Milardovich?

I jumped up and hugged Mom before that last thought could take hold. Then I lifted Nick's gifts from under the tree. "He said we should open these with the rest," I told her.

Mom read the card Nick had taped to her package and I noticed she put it safely on the mantle before she tore off the foil wrap. I remembered that it said, "To Caroline with love from Nick."

The little plastic box inside held four tapes. A gold ribbon that slanted across the top said DANCE TIME, and a tag listed the tunes and the groups. I checked. "The Grateful Dead," "Big Brother and the Holding Company."

"Hey!" I said. "Were these the top names in your day?"

"They sure were."

I noticed that Donovan wasn't listed here and I decided she'd told Nick that Donovan was Dad's and her favorite. I was glad he hadn't tried to jump in on that.

"Here's Nick's gift to you," Mom said.

It was a photograph of Mom's Christmas bike, so glossy, so sharp, it could have been an ad from *Sports Illustrated* or *Bike World.* It had been taken since I'd put on the Campies.

"I wasn't in on the entire secret," Mom said, "but I knew you were getting a photograph and that it had to be a rush job. Nick spent yesterday in the lab at school, developing it and I guess doing the framing and matting."

"Oh." I ran my finger around the dark-blue frame. The color was perfect, showing off the undertones in the black paint.

"*That* must have been what he was up to in the garage. *That's* why he didn't want me to tell you. He was taking this picture."

I felt silly and something else. Maybe ashamed. It was his camera he'd had behind his back! I decided I owed Nick an apology.

The neat label on the back said THIS BICYCLE BUILT BY MARCUS MULLEN AS A GIFT FOR HIS MOTHER AT CHRISTMAS. Underneath was the date. Nick seems to label his pictures on the back, like any good photographer. Anne and Blake. Nick, Anne, and Blake.

"I like it," I told Mom.

She nodded. "It's beautiful. It really does the bike justice. He was going to give you a watch because he noticed you didn't have one, but I told him that . . ."

"What?"

"Oh, that your dad's watch would be yours before too long, and I asked him if he wanted to get you an inexpensive one to fill in till then, but he said no. He never wants to intrude on special things between you and your dad." She smiled at me in a teary kind of way and then said, "So I asked myself why should you have to wait. You're old enough and sensible enough now. I decided you should have your father's watch this Christmas. It's time."

She gave me a small gift-wrapped package. I opened the velvet box inside and took out the watch.

"Put it on, Marcus."

When I pulled the strap to its tightest, it fit my wrist. This was the size Dad's wrist had been at the end. I stood looking down at it, feeling very close to him.

Mom touched my hair. "OK?"

I blinked away the tears. "OK."

"Now. We're not going to be sad at Christmas. Let's open the rest of the things."

I got a card with twenty dollars in it from Grandma, and Grandpa Mullen sent me two great-looking books: *The Cay* and *The Whipping Boy.* Aunt Charlie sent a construction kit so I could make my own radio. The print on the box said *It plays. It's supersonic. It really works.* I decided Aunt Charlie had a lot of faith to think I could ever put it together. Miss Sarah and Miss Coriander had knitted matching sweaters for Mom and me, red with a yellow diamond pattern.

"Are we going to look spiffo or what?" Mom asked me, holding her sweater against her. She sat on the rug, surrounded by torn wrapping and cards. Not Nick's card, though. It was special. I knew that and I knew why, but I felt good anyway.

Robbie had bought me a chef's hat and an apron that said WHAT'S COOKING? in big red letters across my stomach. He was right. It wasn't ordinary.

"You certainly got a lot of nice things," Mom said, and I said, "Yeah. And I got stamps from Anjelica. You know, the girl we met in the mall?"

"Well!" Mom smiled. "Are you sure *you* didn't take my roses? Anjelica, huh?"

Luckily, just then we heard the putt putt of the big car in the driveway next door.

I looked at my watch. Dad's watch. "Ten minutes to twelve," I said. "Miss Sarah and Miss Coriander are off to midnight mass."

The last tape was coming to an end with

readings from Westminster Abbey, and Mom and I sat together, listening to the old familiar words that will always mean Christmas. When the clock struck midnight, Mom put her arms around me and pulled me against her shoulder.

"Merry Christmas, Marky," she said.

"Merry Christmas, Mom."

CHAPTER

14

I got into my pajamas and puttered around my room a bit, putting stuff away. For some reason I didn't feel like going to bed and I definitely wasn't sleepy. When I was little I believed Santa would be creeping into my room at this time on Christmas morning, making sure I was asleep before he filled up my big red sock. And I'd have been struggling to stay awake so I could catch a glimpse of him.

But it sure wasn't the hope of seeing Santa that kept me awake tonight. Too many things on my mind, too much jumbled around in my head. The missing sleeping bag, Nick, the gift giving. I looked at my bike picture. What had he done with the one he'd taken of Mom?

"His Christmas gift to himself," I said out loud. "Because he loves her." I knew it and I knew I was beginning to accept it. There was nothing else to do.

I thought about Anjelica and I wished I'd told Mom about her being here. I couldn't decide why I hadn't. In a way I wished I'd told Mom about the sleeping bag too. Well, I hadn't told that either. It didn't matter.

My stamp album was in the drawer of my desk. I got it out. Then I emptied Anjelica's stamps from their envelope, lined them up in front of me, and went carefully through my album, page by page. Every single one was a duplicate. That made me sad, especially when I remembered how she'd saved them for me all year. Working carefully I took out all the repeats I had, replaced them with Anjelica's and put my originals back in her envelope. There!

It must be about one thirty A.M., I decided. Miss Coriander and Miss Sarah's car had lumbered up the driveway a half hour ago. Christmas morning, and midnight mass over. Everyone would have stood around on the sidewalk outside the church with its big lighted candle in the window, wishing each other Merry Christmas, teary and happy the way people always are after midnight mass. I could still remember. Mom had stopped going when Dad got sick, and she'd never started again. Maybe she would if she and Nick . . .

I clicked off my lamp, got into bed, and lay, watching the moon shadows pale as ghosts on my ceiling, counting on my fingers the things I knew for certain had been taken. My sleeping bag, Mom's clock, the flashlight, food. Wait a sec! I propped myself up on my elbow. Across the room, my mirrored self looked back at me, a pale shimmering blur. Sleeping bag, flashlight, clock, food—it sounded like supplies for a camping trip! Someone going off who didn't have the right equipment and didn't— Hey! What about my pup tent? It was always kept in the left-hand corner of the garage, covered with spiderwebs and dust. It had been there so long that I didn't notice it anymore. Was it still there?

I sat up, lay down again. I'd check in the morning, because if it had disappeared too, I was on the right track. Maybe this meant it had been a kid. No grown-up, real thief would take that kind of stuff and leave money and watches. He could even have had the stereo and the TV. The thought that it might be a kid didn't seem so scary.

I punched up my pillows and turned my face to the wall. Had that tent been there when Robbie and I went over the garage stuff? Today, with Anjelica? I hadn't paid attention to anything when she was there, except her. *IWAKFC!* If I was going to lie here awake I should concentrate on figuring out what that meant, not hassle my head about this other stuff.

But what about the tent?

The last time I'd used it, Robbie and I'd slept in his backyard under the plum tree and plums fell on us all night long. At first we thought it was bird droppings but pretty soon we figured it out.

"A purple-pitted pup tent!" Robbie had said in the morning.

Had the guy taken it? No way was I going to be able to sleep without knowing for sure.

I got up, went down the hallway past Mom's half-open door, past the dining room with its bare, empty table, bigger with the extra leaves we'd put in so we'd all have room at dinner-time. What were those faint creaking sounds? I stopped, listening. The creaking stopped too. Maybe the floorboards in here were squeaky and I'd never noticed. I tiptoed on. Then I heard the creaking again.

I was in the kitchen, the linoleum cold and clammy under my bare feet. No sounds now. Nothing but the night quiet and the *chirp chirp* of a mockingbird in the tree outside. My chest was bursting, my ears ached from listening. Silence.

I was just about to take another step when I heard a small thud, soft and muffled. It came from the laundry room. Someone was in there, not five feet from where I stood. The cold clamminess was all over me now. Thoughts started inside my head and never finished themselves. How did he get in? What was he doing? Should I run back and wake up Mom? Should I yell? If only I had the blackthorn stick I could . . .

The wooden block with our kitchen knives stuck in it was on the counter. All I had to do was slide out a knife. But I could never use a knife, not on anybody, not for any reason. The wooden cutting board was beside it, small and square with a sturdy handle. Could I hit someone with this if I had to? If I had to. But I wouldn't have to. I'd take one quick look and retreat. I picked up the board and went soundlessly forward, carefully, very carefully easing my head around the door.

The laundry-room window was a rectangle of dusty moonlight, the washer and dryer two cubes of reflecting light. A figure stood with his back to me at the bottom of the steps that came down from the attic. His hands still gripped the upper rungs. He'd been up there. The creaking had been him coming down. He'd been up there all the time. That was what I'd been sensing, feeling.

I was shivering as if I had flu and I sucked in a deep, quivery breath and tightened my grip on the handle of the cutting board. He was small, this person. He probably wasn't any bigger than I am. That gave me courage. If he'd been a big guy, a monster guy . . . I licked my dry lips. What I had to do now was leap forward and—

You can't hear someone lick his lips, so it had to be that he sensed me behind him. He spun around, and we were looking directly at each other. T-shirt, jeans, bare feet. One side of him was in moonlight, the other in shadow.

"You've been staying up there, haven't you?" I whispered. "You've been there for days and days." My voice was rising in spite of myself.

He put a finger to his lips.

"Sh!" he whispered.

I'd never seen him before in my life, not in person, but I knew who he was.

CHAPTER

15

I couldn't believe my eyes. "You're Blake," I whispered. "Blake Milardovich. Nick's son."

"Yes. But how do you—"

I interrupted. "Your dad has photographs."

"Oh." He stiffened, like a scared animal, while a car went slowly past on the street outside.

"I have to use the bathroom," he whispered. "Please don't go for your mom . . . please! Can you let me talk to you first?"

I nodded.

"Promise?"

I nodded again. I heard him in the little bathroom and remembered the green footprints . . . his! He'd been the one all the time.

"Sorry I can't flush," he whispered when he

came back. "I can only do that when you're out." Behind us in the kitchen the clock gave its usual hiccup and Blake jumped. "That clock's been giving me heart attacks for days," he whispered. "Could I get something to eat?"

"Sure. What do you want?" I stood aside so he could get past me.

He headed for the cupboard where the cereal is kept, got a dish, went for milk. In the wedge of light from the open refrigerator I saw how dirty he was, the red T-shirt stained, his jeans gray with attic dust, dirt clotted in his hair. His feet were black, blackest between the toes. Knobby feet, like Nick's. He started to eat the cereal before the door closed.

"Here!" I grabbed three bran muffins, all that were left in the package, and held them toward him. "I don't understand why you didn't just go up to Nick's apartment. Nick . . . I mean, your dad would have been so happy."

"Oh sure," Blake said. "He'd have been—"

"Marky!" That was my mother calling.

Blake bumped the cereal dish on the table and I grabbed it up, spilling oat crispies over the floor.

"Coming!" I yelled and started off fast for Mom's room.

She was sitting up, and as soon as she saw me she switched on her lamp. "Why aren't you sleeping? What time is it?"

"About two, I think." I looked down at the cereal bowl.

"You *can't* be hungry," Mom said, and then she smiled and lay down again. "OK, OK. You can always be hungry."

"Do you want something?" I asked.

She shook her head. "And you hurry up and get back into bed. Count sheep or something."

"I will. Good night, Mom."

Blake was in the laundry room again, his back pressed tightly against the wall beside the dryer.

"It's OK," I whispered. "I've thought of a place where we can go to talk."

I gave him the cereal, took the muffins, then carefully opened the door between house and garage.

He followed me into Mom's car, with him behind the wheel and me in the passenger seat. It was cold and very dark. I switched on the dashboard light and reached into the backseat where Mom keeps the old tartan blanket.

"Here." I shared it with Blake. He'd dripped milk down his front in the dark, and I got him the box of tissues, too. There was no point trying to question him while he ate, but that didn't take long. "You want more?" I asked.

He shook his head. "That's OK. I had some crackers earlier when you and your mom went out. And I took a can of tuna from the back of the cupboard. If I go way to the back I figure neither of you will notice. I stole some meat loaf a while back. Yesterday I had a can of stew."

"And peanut butter," I said.

He nodded. "You knew?"

"Not really. How long have you been up there anyway?"

"Five days."

"Five days? Holy smoke! Why?" I asked. "What are you trying to prove?"

"I came to find my father. My name is Miller now. I knew it had been Milardovich because my mom got a letter addressed to that name once. When I asked her about it she said she changed it. Miller was easier. But she acted angry. I figured it out."

"She didn't want your father to find you?"

"No. She said we were hiding because he'd been bad to her, and to me. I was just six. He was glad when the judge gave me to Mom because he never liked me, but she knew he'd be mad because we took off and—" I could see his hands, clenched tight on the steering wheel.

"Wait a sec," I said. "I'm not saying your mom was lying, but she made a mistake in some of that. Nick *did* like you. He liked you a lot. He . . ." I remembered the photographs. I remembered the wrapped gifts from all those Christmases past, and Mom saying how Nick had searched and searched. I remembered Robbie's cousin Jimmy, and how mad Nick had been at the bullying assistant coach, mad enough to fire him even. I remembered the way Nick always was with old Patchin. "I don't believe Nick would ever be bad to anybody, Blake. I honestly don't. And he *did* try to find you. He'll be so jazzed—"

"I haven't decided yet."

"What do you mean?"

"I haven't decided what I'm going to do. I might just go home again."

"That's crazy. Where's home, anyway?"

"San Jose."

"San Jose? How on earth did you find Nick from there?"

"He was on TV when his team won the championship. Coach Milardovich. The La Costa Cougars. I remembered how he looked, sort of. Like me, in a way." Blake glanced quickly at me, then went back to watching his fingers tap the steering wheel. "Funny, I can't remember any of the bad things Mom says he did. Just the good things. Mom says I've blanked out the bad ones. Anyway, I came. I called Information."

"Does your mom know you're here?"

"Mom? Are you crazy?"

"But you've been gone for over five days. She'll be berserk by now." I began kicking off the blanket, feeling I should run and call her right away.

"She won't be berserk. She's in Mexico City for Christmas, with Stanley. Stanley's her friend. They were going to take me . . . happy to take me. . . ." Blake rolled his eyes. "Happier when I told them my buddy J.D. had asked me to spend Christmas with him. In a cabin, in Big Bear."

"She'll check."

"She can't. I told her there's no phone."

"But didn't she call J.D.'s mother?"

"No."

"Oh. Well, I bet she would have called you on Christmas Day."

Blake shrugged. "Maybe. Anyway, I got a bus ticket to LA. Then I hitched here."

"You *hitched?*"

"Sure. Why not? I was out of money. I slept under a tree in that park on the edge of town the first night." He gave me a sideways glance. "Man, there are some weirdos who sleep in that park."

I shivered and pulled the blanket higher on my shoulders. I didn't even want to think about the kind of weirdos there'd be in that park.

"The next morning I came to your house. I was hiding in the bushes and saw you leave your key. At first I thought my father had married again and you were his kid. It took me a while to figure out how things were and that he was in the apartment. Man!"

I rolled the window a quarter inch and tried not to breathe too deeply. This guy smelled of dust and cobwebs and not having washed in a week.

"I sure stink, don't I?" Blake grinned. "Sorry."

"It's OK."

"I tried to get up to my father's apartment a couple of times, but there are these two women who live next door."

"Miss Coriander and Miss Sarah," I said automatically.

"It was impossible. If you weren't here, they were there, like a couple of watchdogs."

"But five days!" I shivered.

"I came down a lot. I even went outside. The air felt great. You almost caught me tonight, though. I just had time to blow out my candle and get behind that cedar closet."

"The candle! That's what I smelled. But how long were you going to stay there, Blake? Forever?"

"Till the day after Christmas. I couldn't leave before that. I have no money and no place to go. Not till Mom gets back."

"And you're honestly thinking of leaving without telling Nick?"

"Maybe."

I thought having the dashboard light on so long might run down Mom's battery, so I switched it off and we sat silently in the dark. The dark was easier.

"Look," I said at last. "I'll tell you one thing. If I had a dad, a real, live dad, I'd never stay away from him. A father is special. . . . I mean, a mom is too. Mine and probably yours." I wasn't sure about his but I thought I should include her. "If I had a dad I'd go to him. Why don't you give Nick a chance?"

Blake didn't answer.

I squinted at the outline of the workbench. "I guess you didn't need the purple-pitted tent," I said.

"What?"

"Nothing. I didn't see my sleeping bag in the attic."

"I kept it in the trunk that's up there when I wasn't using it. It's a pretty good bag. Thanks for lending it."

"You're welcome."

"Thanks for the clock and flashlight too." I

nodded, although he couldn't see me. We sat some more.

"What are you going to do?" I bent to rub one of my icy feet.

Beside me Blake's leg jiggled, from cold or from being scared.

"What are *you* going to do?"

"I'll have to tell my mom."

"She'll tell my father."

"I think she will. Course you never can figure with adults. But I think she will."

His leg jiggling had stopped. "Are she and my dad going to get married?"

"I don't know."

"Is he nice?" Blake asked. "Would you like him for a father, if you were me?"

"I'd like him," I said.

CHAPTER 16

It was four thirty on Christmas morning when Mom called Nick. It hadn't been easy to get her to understand, and she'd kept saying, "In the attic? In *our* attic? Nick's son?" And then, "You poor kid. All alone up there." She'd hugged him hard, not seeming to care about the way he looked or smelled.

On the phone she didn't tell Nick why she wanted him right away, only that it was very important. I guess he could have figured that for himself at four thirty A.M.

"What am I going to say to him?" Blake whispered to me. Mom had asked him if he wanted to wash up, which he did, and she gave him a brush for his hair. It was as thick and curly as Nick's.

"Just say hello," I said. "That's all."

"Do I have to say 'Hello Dad'?"

"Not unless you feel like it," I said.

It was odd the way *I* felt. Pleased for both of them, sure. Antsy because I wasn't sure how it would all come out. A bit embarrassed about being here for the meeting, but knowing we had to stay because Blake asked us to. And there was something else. I was sad. Sad because some guys can lose a dad and get him back and not even know for sure if that's what they want. And some guys can lose a dad and that's all there is to it. The end. Fini. Forever and ever.

We'd left the front door wide open, and we stood in the hallway. Nick came at a rush, blinking in the light, calling Mom's name. He hadn't even stopped to put on a bathrobe, and there he was in dark red pajamas staring at the three of us, Mom in the middle with one arm around Blake and the other around me.

"Blake?" Nick asked. Such a soft, disbelieving whisper for such a big, furry creature. He took a couple of shaky steps toward us and Blake took a couple of shaky steps toward him, and I guess nobody needed to say anything because the two of them were tangled up together in some sort of bear hug. One of them was sobbing.

"So we'll set another place for Christmas dinner," Mom said. She and I were sitting at the kitchen table, talking and drinking apple juice. Blake and Nick had gone up to Nick's apartment "to start filling in some of the gaps," as Nick said.

"What a Christmas present for Nick," Mom said softly. Her eyes were shining.

"Will he get to keep Blake, do you think?"

"I imagine that will be up to some court and judge," Mom said. "And Blake may have a say in it, too."

"I don't like his mother," I said. "She doesn't deserve to have him."

Mom reached out and touched my hair. "Don't judge too harshly, Marcus. They probably hurt each other a lot. Just be happy with Nick that this Christmas morning he is with his son."

Mom made me go lie down for a couple of hours after that while she went next door to talk to Miss Coriander and Miss Sarah. I could just imagine their incredulous gaspings and gulpings. "A child in the house all that time and we didn't know? We must be losing it altogether, Coriander."

I'd told Mom I wouldn't be able to sleep, but I did, and I had a hard time waking when she shook my shoulder at ten. She said that Blake and Nick were still up in the apartment and that it was time to call Minnesota and wish Grandma a merry Christmas, the way we did every year. Mom said we should do that no matter what. After that we called Grandpa Mullen, who lives in a church home in Florida. Aunt Charlie was spending the day with him. He said it was 83 degrees in Florida and could we beat that? We said no, it was forecast to be only 81 in California today, and he gave a great crow of triumph. Grandpa Mullen is very competitive.

All the time I was talking and smelling the good smells of our turkey cooking, I was watching the apartment steps, waiting for Nick or Blake to appear.

I thought about how it would be telling Robbie who'd been in our attic. I'd make him guess. He never would, not in a million years.

I thought it was Robbie later when the phone rang.

"Hello."

"Hello!" Right away I recognized Anjelica's voice, but before I could even say "Merry Christmas," she gasped, "I want a kiss for Christmas, *IWAKFC*," and hung up. I hung up too and wiped my sweaty hands on my jeans. *That* was what it meant. She wanted a kiss from me! Well, Christmas was almost over. I wouldn't see her and I couldn't decide if that was a relief or a disappointment. Anyway, there'd always be next Christmas.

I glanced out the window one more time and saw Nick and Blake coming down the apartment steps. Nick had a Frisbee. Blake was wearing a new blue sweatshirt that must have come out of one of those Christmas boxes. The dust had been brushed off his jeans, and his hair was damp and hanging in dumb little curls, the way Nick's does.

They went on the grass and began throwing the Frisbee back and forth. Across the street Patchin looked up and decided to amble over to join them.

I went to the door.

"Hey, Marcus!" Nick yelled. "Want to play?"

"Sure," I said.

"Call your mom."

I did. And the four of us and Patchin played together for a long time under the Christmas sun.